ABSOLUTION

THE EDITED GENOME TRILOGY BOOK 3

MARCOS ANTONIO HERNANDEZ

ISBN-13: 978-1-7348437-2-9 (Paperback edition)

ISBN-13: 978-1-7348437-1-2 (Ebook edition)

CHAPTER ONE

THERE IS a distinct difference between killing someone and letting them die.

What if the person destined for expiration is in pain? Letting them die could be a mercy. And if the person will be the cause of someone else's pain in the future? The mercy extends to those who would be affected.

Time will tell, and time has no voice.

Shada watched Chloe on the tram, waiting for the poison present in her friend's system to take its toll. She had destroyed the antidote and knew there wasn't long before her friend found out.

Could death be the ultimate escape? Chloe would no longer have to struggle, no longer have to remember, and this in and of itself could be Shada's final gift to her.

The tram sped along the track towards WestCorp's island headquarters, where everyone's genomes were edited to make them happier, healthier, and smarter. Shada and Chloe were headed back to where it had all begun, where, excited at the prospect of their new futures, they'd first arrived to have their own genetic codes edited. Instead, they'd both ended up hosting the minds of now-dead edited humans. Shada reminisced about this trip, the first time they'd met. Chloe, her face dotted with piercings, had been ready to escape the rat race by signing a contract for twenty years of employment on the island in exchange for her edits. Shada's future playing the sport she loved had been ripped away because of a small mutation in her DNA, and she was prepared to sign the same contract and work for the company to help her sister and begin paying down her debt.

The certainty of being happier because of the edits was icing on the cake for both, a way to gain control over their emotions by eliminating the negative ones from existence. But they'd never thought experiencing those negative emotions would be desirable for those who were born without them.

Shada was pulled from her memory when she heard Michael Hollis, the former leader of WestCorp whose mind now resided in her body, cackle in the furthest recesses of her mind. She wondered if he'd influenced her decision to toss the antidote, Chloe's antidote, onto the tracks. Together, they were on their way to kill Michael's wife, Ruby. Could Hollis's captured mind, inside Shada, have been scheming a way to save the woman's life?

Shada wasn't sure she had made the decision on her own.

Tears of blood leaked from Chloe's pale blue eyes, and she wiped them away with the back of her hand. Shada's friend, who had submitted to the implant of a second mind, realized the poison was taking hold, and she looked at Shada with confused eyes.

"You should sit down," Shada said.

Chloe studied Shada's face and a thin smile spread across her lips. Then she said, in a deep voice Shada recognized as the edited mind in control of her friend's body, that someone had switched the antidote.

Shada nodded.

Chloe placed her backpack on the seat next to her with a dull thud from the weight of the gun inside. She then lay on the floor of the tram with her hands across her chest. "Why?" she asked.

"You had to be stopped," Shada replied.

"Stopped? We were in this together!" Chloe said.

"You wanted to eliminate the edited. They're humans too. You seem to have forgotten that."

Once Chloe's plan had been put into motion, her death seemed, to Shada, the most obvious way to terminate it. If Shada hadn't taken action, she felt she would be no better than the edited, whose plan was to force the unedited humans to destroy themselves.

Chloe closed her eyes. A moment passed, then she croaked, "When?"

Shada knew she was referring to how the antidote had gotten switched. She told her friend how she had taken the antidote while Chloe was in the bathroom, then confessed to throwing it on the tracks. She knelt down next to Chloe, who opened her eyes. More blood leaked out and caught in her eyelashes, macabre red mascara.

"You have to capture as many minds as possible," Chloe urged.

A wave of nausea washed over Shada. She already had two minds residing in her body, hers and Michael Hollis's, and the thought of trying to maintain an equilibrium with a third, or fourth, was a burden she didn't want to bear. "It doesn't work like that," she said.

"Do this, for me. I'm not saying you have to eliminate the edited, but the more minds you can gather, the more you can help. Think about your sister, create the world for her."

Shada bristled at the mention of Sikya and took a deep breath to focus herself.

"Alfie will help. He's the only one who knows it's even possible," Chloe said, referring to Alfie Reynolds-Grant, the head scientist for WestCorp and the intellectual leader on the island.

"You put too much faith in him," Shada said.

"What other choice do you have? You're already headed to the island."

"I know," Shada said with resignation. She thought about Ruby Hollis, left in charge of the company when her husband's mind was captured by Shada. Ruby had been hunting Shada in search of revenge and would be grateful when her quarry showed up on her doorstep.

Shada looked through the window as the tram emerged into daylight and watched the approach of the distorted outline of the corporation's compound as they crossed the bridge that spanned the bay. "They're going to be waiting for me," she said.

"Is it possible to send the tram back to the city?" Chloe said, her eyes on the ceiling.

"Of course," Chloe said right away, in a deeper voice.

Shada knew her friend wasn't talking to her, that she was communicating with the captured mind of the island's former head of security, trapped inside her head. Together, she and Chloe had figured out that speaking questions out loud was the best way to get answers from the gatekeeper, whose modified DNA made him unable to maintain an internal dialogue. Shada appreciated the beauty of WestCorp's design, to make sure any of the massive security personnel's thoughts were said out loud. In possession of superior strength and size, they could wreak havoc for the island's inhabitants if they were allowed to plot amongst themselves.

Chloe set her jaw, turned over, and clawed towards an interface next to the door. She stood up and leaned against the wall for support, smearing the surface with blood. "Reverse it," she said.

The tram continued to barrel towards the island while Chloe stood still.

Going back to the city didn't solve Shada's problem. When she and Chloe had pulled out of the station, they'd left behind a group of people who wanted to tear Shada apart. Ruby had edited them, for free, to be angry and impulsive, then informed them Shada was to blame. A powder keg of people had been sent back to the mainland city to find and destroy her, with the fuse lit by Ruby. The one reason returning to the city was better than returning to the island was that Tony and Gustavo, members of a group dedicated to combating the spread of West-Corp's reach, had stayed behind on the platform to fight the horde. Their efforts had given the two women time to escape. Shada might have a chance of survival if those two were still alive.

"Shada's going there to attack Ruby. You're supposed to protect the island," Chloe said to the mind of the gatekeeper in her head.

A moment later, Chloe's hand rose up and pressed a series of buttons, stopping the tram, before another series of buttons sent them back in the direction from where they'd come. She collapsed.

Shada knelt next to her. "I'm sorry," she said, and meant it.

"You did what you thought was right."

Shada realized she had a third option. Her choice of where to go wasn't black or white, life or death, and she wished she could have discovered a third option for Chloe before she'd destroyed the antidote. "There are people on the platform who want revenge," she said as she retrieved the gun from Chloe's backpack before returning to Chloe's side.

"Tony and Gustavo are there to help you." Chloe closed her eyes and sighed. "Think about what you could do with multiple edited minds uploaded into you. You don't want to eliminate the edited? Then don't. But don't squander your gift. Do what you were made to do and change the world."

Shada felt tears well up, and she turned before they could fall. The buildings along the water's edge cast shadows onto the bay, imposing pillars of metal she would have to pass beneath if she wanted to return. "The city was created because humans worked together," she said, her voice drifting off. It struck her how the sprawl had grown over generations to become an amorphous blob. "Without direction," she added. How much better could it be if someone had taken charge?

"You can provide it. Both sides just need someone to bridge the gap," Chloe managed to choke out. Her breathing was labored, and the strain from trying to take in oxygen turned her into a pale white specter writhing on the floor, her closed eyes making her form seem even less human.

Shada stood, cocked the gun, and fired at the window. Air rushed through the shattered glass. She stood on a pair of seats and kicked away enough glass for her body to pass through the opening. She looked back at her friend, said goodbye, and jumped.

CHAPTER TWO

Wɪɴᴅ ʀᴜsʜᴇᴅ past Shada's face as she fell. The sudden acceleration caused her breath to catch in her chest. She tried to keep her feet pointed below her, but the speed she'd acquired from riding the train tilted her body backwards. Time stood still for the few seconds of her free fall, and the moment she hit the water, she felt a sharp slap on the back of her legs and her backside.

She plunged deep into the water and threw her hands out to the side in order to arrest her descent. The cold water almost ripped the breath from her body, but with a conscious effort, she was able to keep the air in her lungs. She kicked out the instant she reached her maximum depth, and all four limbs scrambled to work together on her swim back to the surface. She sensed she must be close to the air above and fought the instinct to open her eyes. Her efforts to resurface continued longer than she felt possible, but still surrounded by water, she had no choice but to continue. Panic set in, and she heard Hollis laugh.

An exhale when her head emerged was followed by a shallow inhale and a mouthful of water. Treading water, she opened her eyes, allowing the world around her to come into focus. She was closer to the city than to the island, in the long shadows of the tallest buildings. She was grateful, because she knew nothing good could come from arriving on the island. If she could make it to the city, she at least stood a chance. She took one last look at the island before she began to swim towards the city and witnessed a craft surface halfway between her and land. It was white, with a bubble on top, and as the vehicle sped to her location, she saw the bubble withdraw. Although the boat was far in the distance, she could tell there were two people on board, speeding towards her.

Shada swam towards the city's shoreline. While in motion, she took stock of her situation and noticed her frantic strokes were unsustainable. She had the composure to realize that with a more controlled cadence, she could save energy without sacrificing the time it took for her to cover the distance, so she focused on being smooth and gliding through the water. She knew that this would give her the best chance of success to make it to the city while leaving some energy for her to deal with capture if the boat caught up to her before she reached safety.

The boat caught up with her while the shore was still far off. It blew past her, and the driver positioned the craft perpendicular across her path.

"Climb onto the boat," one of the men on the boat said to her with the confident air of someone used to being in charge. The boat's passengers were both middle-aged men, clean-shaven, and wore matching dark long-sleeved shirts and dark baseball caps.

Shada studied their faces and checked Hollis's memory for any recollection. He didn't know who they were, but she found out their uniform was worn by members of the WestCorp coast guard.

"You don't really have a choice," Hollis said to Shada, the dialogue occurring inside her mind.

Shada shook her head in response to the captured mind, convinced there was another option. The two men on the boat assumed her gesture was directed at them. The man who wasn't driving reached down, pulled out a wide-barreled weapon, and pointed it at her. "We can do this the hard way if you want," he said with a sneer.

Shada laughed despite her exhaustion. Keeping her head above water was wearing her out, and she knew she couldn't do it for much longer. She was grateful she'd learned to swim when she was young but knew she was so out of practice that her inefficiency was forcing her to work harder than necessary. "Are you going to harpoon me?" she said, even though she didn't see a projectile emerging from the barrel.

The driver of the boat laughed. The man holding the weapon told her, his tone serious, he would shoot the net over her. "Hopefully you don't drown. But don't worry, we'll fish you out."

"Wouldn't be the first time," the driver added.

It was obvious to Shada she had to climb on the boat, but she wanted to maintain her defiance a bit longer. She stared at the two men while treading water, and after a few seconds gave them a tiny nod. The man let the end of the weapon fall as Shada began to swim towards the boat. When she reached the edge, they grabbed a hold of her, one hand beneath each of her armpits, and pulled her up. The moment she collapsed into the boat, a small gun was pressed against her upper arm, the trigger pulled, and she felt the sharp pain of a quick injection. Her surroundings faded from sight.

Shada had no idea how much time had passed before she heard Hollis say, "That was unpleasant." Her eyes were still closed. She'd had no sense of awareness before hearing the captured mind communicate with her, and she wondered if Hollis had been active while she was passed out or if he'd come back from the darkness the exact moment she did. A sobering thought gripped her: What if Hollis became the first object of her awareness every time she woke up? He had access to the space between sleep and wakefulness, between dreams and reality, and if he wanted, he could haunt these times without restriction.

"Sounds like a lot of work," Hollis replied.

Shada hated when he listened to her internal dialogue. She had learned how to keep her thoughts hidden from him, but in her transition state she didn't use the skill. She never bothered trying to block his access to the sensory input of the world around her and wasn't sure she could if she tried. Hollis wasn't able to keep his thoughts hidden from her, evidenced by her ability to probe the full catalog of his memories. As far as she knew, her own memories stayed inaccessible to him, unless he was thumbing through them while she slept, in which case she would never find out.

Red mixed with multicolored spots filled Shada's field of vision, the light beyond her eyes illuminating the blood in her eyelids. She opened her eyes narrow enough that her eyelashes provided a filter against the brightness, and all she could discern was whiteness. She consulted Hollis, asking him instead of probing his knowledge base if he knew where they might be.

"No idea. Definitely on the island though, they wouldn't let you go," he replied.

Over the course of the next several minutes, she worked up to having her eyes open but never readjusted from her original position of lying on her right side. She discovered she was in a small padded room. The floors, walls, and ceiling in her field of vision were all a bright white and composed of padded squares.

She lay still and took stock of her body. She could tell how weak she was and assumed it was from the events leading up to and on the tram, capped off with the plunge into the bay and subsequent swim. Without any knowledge of the time that had elapsed since those events, she couldn't be sure. Her weakness could just as well be from lack of movement over a long period of time. Or, since the facilities on the island were able to upload a mind into another body, could her captors have kept her unconscious while someone else had control of her? She doubted it, since either she or Hollis would have become aware, even if in the background, but the possibility scared her into greater alertness.

Shada decided the reason for her physical weakness didn't matter, that it was a state to be dealt with, and since there were no physical threats present to deal with, she would worry only if it became an issue.

Sitting up, she realized her clothes had been changed. She was now wearing a white gown, like a patient in a hospital. An inspection of her surroundings revealed that the padding's sole deviations were a small handle and space for the doorframe. Shada crossed her legs and began counting her breaths, focusing on both the inhale and exhale, reconnecting with her body, her way of making sure she kept control of her limbs away from Hollis. When the implanted mind had still been new, before she knew what she was doing, she'd thought Hollis had gained control for good, shutting her off from her own body. She'd responded by trying to kill herself. It didn't work, and in the end she became better for the experience, but she never wanted to let her guard down and lose control again.

Ten breaths passed, then twenty, and over time she lost count, absorbed in being in the present moment, experiencing the sensations passing through her body as they arose. A click rang out, and she opened her eyes.

"Shada. Welcome back," a woman's voice said.

Shada didn't need the captured mind inside her to confirm that the voice belonged to Ruby.

CHAPTER THREE

SHADA LOOKED around the padded room, trying to find a microphone, or a speaker, or a camera. Finding none, she stayed facing the direction she was sitting and talked to the open air around her.

"What do you want?" she said.

"You took something that belongs to us," the bodiless voice of Ruby replied.

Hollis laughed. "I didn't belong to anyone, not even her," he said.

Nobody but Shada could hear his response.

Shada didn't say a word. Her first instinct was to disengage, to wait and see what the woman who held her captive wanted. She heard Ruby sigh into the microphone.

"Look, I know Michael was uploaded into you. But I need to know how much you know about what we do here. Can you read his thoughts? Or have you kept him locked away, banished in the basement?"

Shada wished she knew where the camera was so she could stare into it and still not say a word.

"We can do this the easy way, or the hard way," Ruby said,

exasperated. She sounded like a woman at wit's end, tired of the game.

Something in Ruby's voice made Shada decide to cooperate. She'd never planned to be back on the island and had no energy to resist any longer. "I can," she said, admitting she could access the memories of the former leader of the island corporation.

There was a momentary silence before Ruby spoke again. "Where did we meet?"

"I believe you were in Chloe's body and brushed my cheek when we were in Hollis's office."

"Not you and me, idiot," Ruby snarled. "Michael and I."

Shada delved into the catalog of Hollis's memories, searching for the first time they met. "You two were in school together, on the island. You were a few years younger than him, but he knew who you were. Your meeting was arranged by WestCorp as a potential match, for breeding purposes. You had two children and raised them in a house by the water."

Shada's account of Michael and Ruby's past was met with silence. It must have been enough to satisfy Ruby, because when she spoke again, she asked Shada what her favorite flower was.

Hollis himself supplied the answer. "She never liked flowers, thought they were frivolous," he told Shada. Shada relayed the message to the empty room.

"So you know everything about WestCorp," Ruby said, her voice trailing off.

"Or can find out. To be honest, I haven't bothered to investigate because I don't care. I tried to leave what you do, or did, on the island behind. I assume there have been some changes since you've been in charge."

"There have been a few," Ruby admitted.

"He didn't know about this room, for one," Shada admitted.

"It's new. Built in case we got a hold of you. If you wanted to leave the island behind, why did you come back?"

It was a good question, one Shada couldn't provide a clear answer to. "Chloe thought it was important."

"But she died on the way here," Ruby said.

"She did." From the tone of Ruby's voice, Shada guessed the woman didn't know she was the one who'd allowed Chloe to die by destroying the antidote. She again wondered how much time had passed since she'd been pulled from the water and if the tram car holding Chloe's body had been returned to the island, the body removed, and the window fixed.

There was a click, and Shada knew the conversation was finished. She sat up and returned to counting her breaths. The breath work was a gateway into the true source of her control over Hollis: the ability to find her heartbeat and follow its resonance to every limb in her body. The low dose of modified LSD provided by Alfie, designed to allow Hollis to maintain control, had exposed Shada to the concept and resulted in Hollis losing control of her body for good. The resonance of her heartbeat had first surfaced in the presence of other unedited humans, the synchronization making her own heartbeat easier to detect, but after practicing while she was in hiding from WestCorp, she had learned to focus on its steady rhythm alone and without the drug.

After an unknown length of time, the door opened, and one of the massive humans bred to be a security guard—the same type of edited human whose mind had been Chloe's second upload—walked in. He appeared unsure of his footing; each step was taken with a deliberateness bordering on caution. Shada realized he was bracing himself for action every time both feet were on the ground, assuming she might run or attack, even though he was bigger than Shada by half. In his hand was a large clear glass containing a thick white liquid, which he held out to Shada without saying a word.

"What is it?" Shada asked. She took the glass for the simple reason it was held out for her to take.

"Drink," the giant grunted.

Shada smelled the liquid and detected sweet hints of vanilla. Still seated, she looked into the guard's face. His features were oversized, like the rest of his body, with an enormous round nose, deep-set eyes, a heavy brow, and a large mouth. He nodded with his chin and raised his eyebrows, urging Shada to drink. He didn't smile, but Shada felt the gesture was his form of connecting.

There were four large mouthfuls of liquid to consume, and Shada took them one after the other. The taste wasn't bad, but it had a certain thickness she found off-putting. The guard stayed until Shada finished the drink, then took the glass back with him when he left.

Shada felt sick to her stomach from all the liquid, so she lay down to let it settle. She stayed there a long time, satisfied with existing, and felt herself drifting off to sleep. Whoever was monitoring the prisoner must have been able to tell, because a loud beep rang out from the direction of the door. Nobody ever entered.

It wasn't until the third time this happened that she realized they were keeping her awake. She wondered if, as she got more tired and closer to falling asleep regardless of interruptions, there would be an escalation of methods to complete their assignment. She got her answer after two more occasions of being thrust into wakefulness.

She was determined to fall asleep despite the beep, but the door opened as she drifted off. The change in stimulus was successful, and her eyes watched the opening door while her head stayed still. She assumed it would be one of the massive guards again and was taken aback when she recognized the normal-sized man who walked into her small room. It was Alfie Reynolds-Grant, the head scientist, the man who'd uploaded Hollis's mind into her body and insisted she call him by his first name.

"Alfie!" Shada exclaimed, sitting upright so fast she became dizzy. He had shaved off his beard, but his gray hair looked to be the same length and still had thin wisps sticking out at odd angles.

"Hello, Shada," Alfie said. In his hand was a small gun, the same type as the one used by the men on the boat to tranquilize her.

Shada scrambled away. Her limbs were heavy and movements sluggish. The last time she'd received an injection of this kind, she'd lost track of time and woke up in the padded room.

Alfie approached Shada, staring at her with the kind eyes of a grandfather.

"What's that?" Shada asked, her chin gesturing to the weapon in his hand. The juxtaposition of it in contrast with his demeanor kept her on high alert, uncertain about how to respond.

"Just a quick injection," Alfie said. He took a step forward, and Shada slid along the wall. "Please don't make this more difficult than it has to be," Alfie said. "I can always call one of the guards in here to hold you in place."

Shada's skin crawled at the thought of being touched by one of the massive humans. She set her jaw and withdrew from the wall she was pasted on. When she got close, Alfie held out the gun, and Shada put her upper arm up to the end of the barrel. Alfie pulled the trigger.

Her heart began to race, and her first thought was to get it under control so that Hollis couldn't take over her body. She didn't make any effort to hide her reservations from Hollis, who assured her he wouldn't waste a takeover of her body in a room where he couldn't "do a damned thing."

"What was that?" Shada asked Alfie, her eyes wide. He had made his way to the door and was halfway through.

Alfie paused, leaned back to look at her, and said, "Stim," before walking out.

CHAPTER FOUR

SHADA, sitting against the wall farthest from the door, began a series of rapid breaths in order to give her body somewhere to expend the excess energy caused by the Stim. She consulted with Hollis about the injection device that had twice been used on her, asking him outright instead of taking the time to probe his memories. "They used the same thing to knock me out on the boat," she said.

"It was a prototype when I was still around, simmering on the back burner, to be developed if we needed increased control over visitors from the city," Hollis informed her.

Shada focused on her breathing while waiting for the captured mind inside her to continue.

"The Stim was a different project. The ultimate goal was to create a method for physical labor enhancement, one that each person could shoot into themselves whenever they felt their body was slowing down. Workers would require less sleep and experience maintained or increased output. I suggested we package the substance in independent vials workers could inject themselves, since everyone experiences fatigue at different rates based on food consumption, sleep, and baseline fitness."

"If everyone had an injection gun, it wouldn't be hard to use it on themselves," Shada thought, in response to Hollis.

Before Hollis could respond, the door to Shada's room flung open and a massive guard filled the doorframe. Shada, still taking rapid breaths, met his gaze. The guard grinned with delight and seemed to enjoy watching Shada struggle with the Stim's effects. "Let's go," he said, tilting his head to the right before turning around.

Shada didn't wait for another invitation. She stood up and walked out, following the guard out the door and turning left. She passed a second guard stationed outside her room to the right, and the man began following her. Walking barefoot between the two large humans, she recognized Hollis's underground bunker. She was led to the elevator that would take her to the island's surface; the heavy footsteps of the guards reverberated off the high stone ceilings of the cave.

"They've been busy down here," Hollis told Shada.

"I wonder what they did with your body," Shada thought, communicating with Hollis by thought. The upload of Hollis's mind into Shada had been performed down the hall in the opposite direction, leaving his former body an empty shell. In theory, it could still be kept alive, but what use could someone have for the brain-dead body of a man with a terminal illness?

"Who's to say they haven't kept it warm for me to come back to?" Hollis said with a laugh.

The guards in front of and behind Shada had no idea she was communicating with Hollis. All they heard was her heavy breathing.

The two guards and Shada took the elevator to the surface and walked outside to a sun that was low in the sky. Around the entrance to the bunker was a square area surrounded by a chain-link fence with barbed wire above, and there were four more guards outside the enclosure, one at each corner. Against the fence on the side closest to the sun lay a medium-sized dog, dusty brown with flecks of gray around its face. When it saw people emerge from the bunker, its head lifted and tail wagged.

Shada stopped when the guard in front of her stood on one side of the door. The guard behind her pushed her forward. "Exercise," he said.

She didn't need to be told twice. Turning to the right, she set off at a jog with Stim coursing through her veins. The dog, sensing it was time to play, joined her as she ran back and forth, touching one side of the chain-link fence before turning around and heading towards the opposite side. Each time she turned around, the dog jumped up and got ready to play, under the impression that when Shada turned around the game was about to begin. During one of these jumps, Shada discovered her canine companion was male.

This routine continued until the sun had risen in the sky. By then, her legs felt weak, but pure energy still coursed through her veins. She dropped to the ground and performed push-ups, with the intention of continuing until her arms gave out, but the dog wouldn't leave her alone and kept trying to lick her face. She gave up and began playing with the animal instead. She had never seen a dog outside of a cage on the island, and she wondered if they'd brought it out just for her.

The two of them created a game where she would slap her hands against the ground, and the dog would respond by leaning forward onto his forepaws, keeping his hindquarters high in the air, at which point Shada would crawl forward until their heads came into contact. Over time, the dog got worked up and yelped, at which point one of the guards stationed at the bunker door spoke up for the first time since she'd first walked outside.

"Jax!" the guard said.

The dog's tail dropped, and it slinked away.

"That's enough for today," the guard informed Shada. "Time to go back inside."

Shada stood up and became aware of her dirty hands, feet, and knees. The guards must have noticed too, because instead of taking her back to the padded room, they continued through the bunker to the end of the hall, through the large open space that housed the kitchen and large table, into Hollis's bedroom, which was adjacent to the room where the initial upload had taken place. The door to the upload room was closed, so in theory Hollis's body could still be behind the door.

The guards ushered her into Hollis's bathroom and commanded her to take a shower. She removed her gown and bathed, taking pleasure in watching the brown water disappear down the drain. When she finished, she found her soiled gown had been taken away and a fresh one was hanging on the back of the door.

Shada expected to see the guards outside the bathroom, waiting in Hollis's bedroom, but they weren't there. She was about to look through the space, both out of her own curiosity and to give Hollis the chance to look at his old stuff again, but a woman's voice called out to her from outside the bedroom.

"Shada, are you finished in there?" It was Ruby, her voice full of a sickening artificial sweetness.

Shada's jaw clenched, and a tide of rage surged to her extremities. She didn't allow the feelings to linger, afraid she wouldn't be able to maintain control over Hollis, and she took ten slow breaths to calm down and stay present before walking out.

Ruby was seated next to Alfie in the two chairs closest to Hollis's bedroom. The black stone wall behind them glittered from where the light caught its jagged edges, reminding Shada of numerous stars looking down on her from the night sky. The guards stood on each side of the door to Hollis's bedroom. Ruby gestured to the seat across from her. "Sit down," she said.

Shada knew she had no choice in the matter. Flanked by the two guards, she approached then sat down in the seat she was told to occupy. Both guards stood behind her.

"How are you doing?" Ruby asked.

In an instant, Shada checked in with her body and found the Stim was still keeping her in an elevated state. "What do you want?" she said.

Ruby turned to Alfie. "All business," she said. "I like that."

Alfie shrugged.

She turned back to Shada. "I'm going to need to upload into you to talk to my husband."

Shada stared at Ruby. Unlike Chloe, Shada had never wanted to upload another mind. Her apprehension must have been painted on her face, because Ruby tried to assuage her fears.

"It won't be permanent, not at all! I like my body," Ruby said. "It can be quick, but I need you to agree to it."

"Why? You could just knock me out."

"If you're knocked out, Hollis will be too," Alfie said.

"You could restrain me."

"I've considered it," Ruby admitted. "But you've already demonstrated the ability to keep control over Hollis. If you choose to maintain control and keep us separated, it would be a waste of both our time for me to go inside."

Shada checked in with Hollis while waiting for Ruby to continue. He was curious about what his wife could want to discuss.

"Alfie will make sure we don't go past the agreed-upon length of time. We can do it right there," Ruby said, gesturing to the room where Michael Hollis had uploaded into Shada.

Both Shada and Hollis were curious about what was behind

the closed door, to see if his body had been removed. "If Alfie can guarantee it will only be for an hour," Shada said. "And you'll let me sleep after."

"Two," countered Ruby.

Shada crossed her arms and leaned back.

Ruby studied Shada's face before her shoulders fell and she agreed to one hour. "And no more beeps."

"Let's get it over with," Shada said. Alfie stood up and led Ruby to the upload room, telling Shada he'd call her in when everything was set up.

CHAPTER FIVE

WHATEVER HOPE Shada had had that Ruby would scream at the sight of her husband's brain-dead body evaporated as soon as Alfie and Ruby opened the door. The room was small, so there was no way a dead body could be missed. Minutes ticked by before Alfie told Shada to come inside.

The guards attempted to follow Shada into the small room, but a look from Alfie told them to stay outside. "I'll call you if you're needed," he told them.

Ruby was lying on the same table her husband had been on the last time Shada was inside the room. She already had the modified helmet with its multicolored wires over her head. Her eyes were closed, her arms folded on her chest. With her wrinkles still visible on her resting face, Shada found it hard to believe this was the woman who held her captive.

"You know what to do," Alfie told Shada, using his lips to gesture to the second table.

Shada climbed onto the stainless steel table and put the second modified helmet over her head. Her gown had ridden up and exposed the skin on the backs of her legs to the cold table, but she didn't bother to adjust herself. "One hour," she said.

"One hour," Alfie replied, pushing a series of buttons on a computer between the tables.

Shada crossed her arms over her stomach and closed her eyes. "Let's get this over with," she said.

She didn't have to wait long. Moments later, Alfie initiated the upload, and Shada was plunged into darkness. The process was designed so that the mind of the person being uploaded into would be shoved to the background, forced to exist in a vacuum, while whoever uploaded was free to use the new body as they saw fit. Shada had figured out—and shared the knowledge with Chloe—how to come back from the darkness then use the breath to take initial control back from the uploaded mind. That's what she did the instant she found herself surrounded by darkness.

It was like looking out from the bottom of a well towards a small circle of light in the distance. Instead of moving towards the light, the light had to be allowed to grow larger, like looking at a star in the sky using peripheral vision to sense the absence of darkness instead of staring directly at the light. Once the light grew large enough, the world could be seen through her own eyes, and hearing came once the darkness at the periphery disappeared. With hearing came a small recognition of the breath, and once the breath could be controlled, the body was back in the control of its original owner.

It had taken Shada days to figure this out the first time, and it had almost cost her her life. Chloe had been able to replicate the process twice and seemed to be comfortable doing so. This time, with both Ruby and Michael Hollis uploaded into Shada, and therefore neither of them able to slow her down, the process of coming back from the darkness was instantaneous.

"That was fast," Hollis remarked. "She just got in here!"

"Leave us alone!" Ruby screamed.

"It's no use, honey, she's in control now," Hollis said to his wife. He asked Shada not to hold the outburst against her.

"I don't need or want her forgiveness!" Ruby said, continuing her tantrum.

Shada severed the communication between the two voices in her head and looked at the room around her. Alfie was staring at the monitor. He seemed to sense Shada's gaze and didn't look up from his work.

"It's you, isn't it?" he said.

Shada could tell Alfie was aware of who was in control. "How'd you know?" she asked.

"You're missing that extra sense of wonder," he replied. "When a new upload sees the world through someone else's eyes for the first time, they look around as if seeing the world brand new. You're just looking at me, annoyed."

"She doesn't like not being in control," Shada told the scientist.

"I can imagine."

Shada checked in with the couple. Hollis was silent, waiting for Shada to allow space for him to communicate with his wife, experience having taught him that it was useless to rebel.

Ruby, on the other hand, hurled obscenities at Shada, a stream of insults that Shada found amusing.

"Are you done?" Shada said, interrupting her.

"You agreed, you backstabbing—"

"Stop. It's time for you to agree to something. Let me off the island, and I'll let the two of you talk."

"Let you go?" Ruby said, stalling for time. One thing Ruby didn't realize about being a guest in Shada's mind was that the host could read her thoughts, so even though she was trying to come up with a lie, Shada knew the truth.

"You wanted me to show you it's possible to upload a second

mind," Shada told Ruby. "You have someone in mind you want me to take off your hands."

"Stay out of my head!" Ruby yelled.

"You know, you're the one in my head," Shada countered. "If I agree to upload this other mind, then you'll let me go?"

Ruby gave up pretending to keep her thoughts hidden. "Yes," she said. "If you can do it, I can have Alfie figure out how to do it with others."

Shada probed Ruby's thoughts once more and found out that the mind she wanted implanted into Shada's head was speaking out against actions taken by Ruby and the trajectory of the company under her control. Shada then withdrew and allowed the couple to communicate with each other.

Michael and Ruby Hollis began by discussing all that had occurred on the island since Hollis had left, a rundown of the business since his upload. Shada felt sad that this was the state of their relationship, that they had no personal news to share with each other, and she decided to leave them alone until their time was up.

During the next hour, alone in the room with Alfie, Shada spent her time focused on her breathing, alternating between sitting up and lying down with her eyes closed. The Stim still present in her system wouldn't let her stay in one position for long, and when she was tired of paying such close attention to her breath, she would watch Alfie monitor the status of the upload on the computer monitor. Every time she checked in with the conversation occurring in the background of her mind, she found they were discussing past events at WestCorp and ways Ruby could have better handled the situation. Shada was brought up towards the end of their time together, with Hollis asking what was to be done with her. Ruby didn't go into specifics with her husband but told Hollis she "had a plan," and that he didn't need to worry, which Shada knew from reading

Ruby's thoughts stemmed from the proof that it was possible to capture another mind.

"I know you'll get it taken care of," Hollis said. "Just remember, I'm still in here," he added.

Ruby said she knew, and the conversation died, as if they could tell Shada was listening. In the physical world, Alfie informed Shada it had been an hour, and he told her to lie back down and put the helmet back on.

"Let's get her out of there," he said.

A moment later, both Ruby and Shada sat up and removed their helmets.

"We should talk," Ruby said. Her voice contained none of the anger and frustration she couldn't contain while uploaded.

Shada wondered if there was a constant difference between her internal state and her exterior presentation. "You do know I'm your prisoner, right? You just show up and I don't have a choice whether I want to talk to you or not."

Ruby slid off the table and began to leave. "I'll come back soon," she said before walking out.

Shada was led back to the padded room. She sat in the middle of the room, alone in her amazement at how well she had been able to maintain control of herself with two minds uploaded into her body. She made sure to keep these thoughts hidden from Hollis, because she wanted to sort through how she felt without interference before having to deal with Ruby again.

Had Chloe been right to suggest she upload multiple minds? She had to assume Ruby and Michael Hollis would possess the most potential to disrupt her control, and she had been able to keep their conversation in the background. If there were minds left to their own devices in the background, could they be used to figure out how to create a world where edited and unedited humans could coexist without her involvement? She had never wanted the burden, and didn't think it possible, but after experiencing the ease with which she'd held two minds apart from herself, she couldn't help but extrapolate to three, and four, in the future, all working together for a common goal.

Shada fell asleep in a corner of the padded room. This time there were no beeps to keep her awake. She lost all track of time —not that she was able to track the days in the windowless room —and she was woken up by a guard entering and telling her that Ruby was on her way to see her.

"Let's go," the guard said. He didn't sound rude, even though his direct method of communication could seem so if taken at face value. The words themselves were said with softness, as if he would say more if he could, but he lacked the language to elaborate.

Shada was led back to the large table and given another glass of the thick vanilla meal replacement while she waited. It was finished by the time Ruby arrived, flanked by two more guards.

Ruby sat across from Shada and folded her hands on the table. The two women looked like children compared to the four guards that stood around them.

"So you really did take my husband with you when you left," Ruby said.

Shada nodded. "I really did."

"And you showed you can keep hold of two minds as well."

Shada was about to reply that Chloe could do the same thing, but she wasn't sure whether Ruby knew the extent to which her friend had plotted to eliminate the new leader of WestCorp. Chloe had been Ruby's personal assistant and was working the entire time to destroy the company from the inside.

"Get to the point," Shada said. It was as if Ruby wanted Shada to agree with everything she said, not content to impose her will on someone she knew she couldn't control. At a certain point, the cards had to be laid down so Shada could make a decision about how to act. Whether she agreed or not was a different matter.

"I'm here to discuss your freedom," Ruby replied. "And the taking of another mind with you when you go."

"Did Alfie have anything to say about this?" Shada asked.

"Says there shouldn't be any problems," Ruby replied.

Shada knew Chloe's second upload had been performed without problems, but in time her friend had still ended up dead.

"Do I have a choice?" Shada asked.

"In theory, you could say no, but she's already in there with Alfie," Ruby said, looking at the closed door of the upload room.

CHAPTER SIX

SHADA TURNED around in her chair and stared at the closed door of the upload room. She shook her head. "There's something wrong with you people," she said.

"Funny, we say the same thing about you."

"Let's get this over with then," Shada said, sliding her chair back and standing up. Part of her, a small part, was pleased with herself for saving the mind of someone whom Ruby detested. If she died, her knowledge and memories would evaporate into nothingness, but instead they were now being added to Shada's collection.

The four guards stayed still as Shada walked over to the upload room and opened the door. Alfie looked up from his work, a thin smile on his lips. He nodded to her before putting his head back down and resuming his preparations for the upload.

The woman lying on the table had on the same style gown Shada wore. Her wrinkled arms and legs were spotted with age, and her white hair stuck out from beneath the helmet already covering her head. Her breathing was steady, and she didn't acknowledge that Shada had entered the room.

Alfie, his eyes still down, must have sensed Shada's gaze, because he explained the woman was in an induced coma. "Her body's out, but her mind is still active," Alfie said.

Shada lay down, covered her head with the helmet, and didn't have to wait long until Alfie made the switch. She recovered her senses right away but stayed still so that she could get a sense of how much resistance the woman would have now that she no longer controlled a body.

"What's your name?" Shada asked. She blocked Hollis from their communication. She thought it would be harder to keep the two minds separate during the permanent upload, but her organized mind did it by default.

A small voice responded, full of trepidation. "Marnie," she said.

"Do you have a last name, Marnie?" Shada asked. She could tell she had access to the woman's memories but chose not to probe, at least not yet.

"Marnie Compana," the woman said. "Where am I?"

"You were uploaded into my body," Shada told her.

"Uploaded?"

The uncertainty in the woman's voice made Shada uneasy. "Didn't you know this was going to happen?"

"The doctors told me I needed to be put into a coma, so my body could heal. I assumed I would be going into the dream station."

"The dream station?" Shada asked. She had never heard of the device.

"It's a way for older people to pass the time once we're past working age."

"People on the island?"

"Yes." Something about Shada's question caused Marnie to pause. "Wait," she said, "you aren't edited?"

"No, I'm not."

Shada allowed Hollis into the thought-conversation. "Hollis is edited."

"I am," Hollis said.

"Hollis? As in, Michael Hollis? I assumed you were dead."

"My physical body died, but my mind lives inside this unedited woman."

"What's her name?" Marnie asked Hollis. Then, aware that Shada could also hear her, she redirected the question. "What's your name?"

"Shada Gray. I grew up in the city."

"So you're unedited."

"Correct."

"And who are you?" Hollis asked.

"Marnie Compana." Her response to Hollis was all business, like she was talking to a superior. "I was on the team that works with the city's government, until they phased me out due to age. They put me into a coma, and I assumed I would be taken to the dream station, but instead I woke back up in here."

Shada probed Hollis's memories and discovered that the dream station was how the majority of older edited humans passed their time. Instead of uploading into another person's body, they would spend anywhere from two to six hours inside the device, their minds experiencing everyday activities in a body that wasn't broken down. For most, it was how they passed the time until they died, the one thing they looked forward to each day. As edited humans, they would have been content with simple existence until their death, but this was a way for West-Corp to test the possibility of further productivity for mental tasks.

"This was Ruby's plan," Shada told Marnie.

Marnie laughed. "Doesn't surprise me, she wanted me out of the picture. I knew what she was doing to those poor unedited. They came thinking they were getting the standard edits, the ones everyone on the island receives, and instead they were edited to be worse versions of themselves."

"If you were phased out of your job, why would she care if you knew?" Shada asked.

"Just because I wasn't working day-to-day doesn't mean I didn't have any influence. My protégé came to me to discuss their misgivings with the direction of their work, and I told them to talk to their superior and to stop working if they thought it was best. Of course they didn't listen; the edits allow us to stay in ignorant bliss. Ruby must have found out about my advice and taken steps to drown out the voice of reason."

Shada knew she could discover the identity of the protégé by probing Marnie's mind but chose to let the woman keep the knowledge for herself.

Marnie continued. "Makes me wonder if I even needed to be put into a coma or if it was Ruby's idea. I was sick, no doubt about it, but didn't feel any worse than normal."

"Sounds like something she would do," Hollis admitted.

Shada opened her eyes, ending the meeting of the three minds that occupied her body. She sat up, and Alfie studied her face.

"Everything all right?" Alfie asked, as if he was unsure of who he was talking to.

"Everything's fine," Shada replied.

Alfie's shoulders relaxed the moment he comprehended that Shada was the one in charge. "How'd she take it?"

"She's surprised," Shada said. "But offered no resistance. I haven't even felt her try to take control of my limbs, but if she did, I could stop her."

"Fisher was the same way. Once Chloe took back control, he accepted their arrangement, as far as I'm aware."

Shada didn't want to talk about Chloe. The guilt involved made her second-guess herself, and with multiple minds now under her control, the last thing she needed was a crisis of confidence. "Is Ruby still here?" she said.

"Still outside. It's been all of five minutes."

Shada took the helmet off and set it on the table. "Good, I want to talk to her."

"I believe she wants the same thing."

Shada strode back out into the open space outside the upload room. Two of the guards, the ones who had been with Ruby when Shada arrived, were still standing behind the leader of WestCorp. The two who'd escorted Shada were on the far side of the room, on the opposite side of the massive table, helping themselves to whatever food was in the kitchen. Based on the limited amount of trash on the counter and their empty hands, they hadn't found much.

"Shada?" Ruby said, as if questioning the unedited woman's ability to gain back control over her own body.

"It's me. Marnie's here too."

"Good to hear."

Shada placed both hands on the back of the chair opposite Ruby. "Happy?" she said.

Shada stared at the older woman and watched Ruby close her eyes and nod.

"Marnie put her nose where it didn't belong, that's all. By doing so, she made herself the leading candidate for my second permanent upload test."

"You went in and talked to your husband. That should've been proof enough of what I can do."

"Paying a visit and moving in are two different things. Are you able to keep control over both of them? What's it like? We never talked about my visit, and I'm so curious. I'd upload another mind into myself if I could."

The thought of Ruby displaying enough self-awareness to

keep multiple minds organized made Shada laugh. "I'd like to see you try. Let me in, see if you can keep control."

Ruby was amused by Shada's suggestion.

"Now that you've seen for yourself it's possible, I'm free to go, right? You said this upload was in exchange for my freedom."

"Correct, a deal's a deal. You got rid of a thorn in my side, and now I'll help you. You are free to go."

Shada stood up straight and looked at the stone ceiling above. "Finally!" She looked around. "Now where's my stuff? I'm leaving."

"There's one more thing," Ruby said.

Shada glared at the seated woman. "What?" she said. She had read Ruby's mind while the woman was uploaded and knew there hadn't been more to her plan.

"Let me rephrase: a few more things. There are others on the island who continue to . . . disagree with my methods. You'd think since everyone is edited to be happy, nobody would bother trying to change the status quo."

Shada wondered if Ruby had been able to withhold information from her or if she had thought of this added wrinkle after spending some time alone. Whichever the case, Ruby was dangerous, but if she could keep her thoughts hidden from Shada while uploaded, Shada had to be more cautious when dealing with her in the future.

"What does this have to do with me?" Shada asked. There was no way she would agree to upload another mind, no matter how much Ruby tried to sweeten the deal.

Ruby leaned forward in her chair. "I want you to convince others from the city to come onto the island and leave with the minds uploaded into them."

CHAPTER SEVEN

RUBY STARED AT SHADA, waiting for an answer. The hungry look in her eyes made Shada's hair stand on end.

Shada knew there were unedited inhabitants of the city who would jump at the chance to upload one of the edited minds into their body. One member of the resistance, Richard, had been brought by Chloe to try to accept an edited mind into his body. Shada and Chloe were the only two living humans who had been able to undergo the procedure, and both had been subjected to a temporary occupation before the permanent upload. There must have been something about the experience that prepared them to receive a permanent upload, because Richard, as soon as he regained the tiniest bit of control, ended the experiment by jumping off the roof of a building on the island.

It also helped that Shada had told Chloe how to take back control, sharing her own process with her friend and making sure the procedure was understood. Richard had to hear about the steps secondhand through Chloe, one step away from the source, lessening his chance for success.

Shada knew Tony and Gustavo, Richard's comrades in the

resistance, would jump at Ruby's offer. In their eyes, it would be their chance for revenge, resulting in one less edited human in existence. The acquisition of a lifetime of knowledge and experience that could be referenced and drawn upon whenever needed was a delightful bonus. What did Ruby know about the resistance? She herself didn't know much; it had been Chloe who had the most experience with them. The group had been used by the city's new mayor, Mayor Tensen, to escort Shada and her sister, Sikya, into hiding. The group took care of the logistics. Their plan had worked, until Shada had chosen to come back to the island with Chloe and left Sikya in Chloe's apartment.

What a mistake that had been.

All these thoughts passed through Shada's mind in an instant, and she nodded to Ruby. "If I agree to bring them, then I'm free to go?"

"Correct."

Shada's thoughts turned to Marnie. The woman had taken the transplant of her mind without resistance. If others pushed back, it would be harder for the unedited members of the resistance to control their own bodies, assuming they agreed to the procedure. "I'm not sure they will be able to walk out of here in control of their own bodies," Shada told Ruby.

Ruby leaned back in her chair. "I've thought about that. There are two things working in favor of this new cohort. One, they'll have you to guide them through the steps. I understand you were the first to pull it off, and I'm assuming you told Chloe how to do it?"

Shada nodded.

Ruby continued. "And two, I'm going to tell the edited minds it's their chance for immortality. Might even use Michael as the example. This prospect alone should be enough to convince the selected individuals to go along with the procedure."

"Why are these individuals speaking out against you?"

"They're the ones who advocated for the negative edits," Ruby said with sadness. "I never should have listened to them. You'd be helping all the unedited people by taking their opinions off the island."

Inside Shada's head, Marnie called Ruby a liar. "She's the one who wanted to perform those edits!" she said.

Until Marnie spoke up, Shada hadn't been sure if Marnie was able to experience the outside world or if she was still stuck in the darkness. Shada also knew Ruby was lying but didn't bother contradicting her.

"If they are speaking out against you, why would they trust you enough to go through with the upload?" Shada asked. It was more of a question to herself that she spoke out loud. She realized she could say the same thing about herself. Here she was, entertaining a discussion about the plan, even though she felt Ruby was a snake in the grass ready to strike at any moment.

Ruby sighed. "Everyone wins," she said. "They get taken off my island, and the people who agree to the procedure gain the experiences and knowledge acquired over a lifetime."

"Why not just put them in a coma?" Shada asked. "They won't say a word."

Ruby considered the question for a moment before responding. "It would look too suspicious. If it's their own choice though, nobody would point fingers at me." Ruby looked at the guards around her before continuing. "And I can't just upload all these minds into you, because I don't know what would happen to Michael. To be honest with you, I want to see if your results are repeatable, to see if anyone can learn the skills you and Chloe demonstrated or if the two of you are unique. If I can figure out how to pull off a successful upload with another unedited, then Alfie can develop the technology to make it happen for anyone who wants the procedure."

"And what if I don't agree? I could force Hollis into the darkness right now and you'd never hear from me again," Shada said.

In her mind, Shada heard Hollis curse his wife's name.

"Well, I'll just have to tell the people who receive negative edits that it was Sikya's fault they ended up worse than before."

Shada was stunned. She had nothing more to say. With a threat to her sister now on the table, she knew she had no choice. The disgust in her stomach was as clear a sign as any that it was time to leave the island. With her head down, she informed Ruby she would find people willing to receive the upload. "How many do you need?" she asked.

"Seven," Ruby said as she stood up from her chair. The two guards who had come with her snapped to attention. She beckoned for the two guards who'd retrieved Shada from the padded room to take Shada to get her belongings. "They're in the room next to where you've been staying," Ruby explained, as if the padded room hadn't been used for Shada's imprisonment. Then she left, her footsteps echoing down the long hall towards the elevator.

Shada glimpsed Ruby and her entourage getting onto the elevator in the distance before she was led into Hollis's study. Hollis begged Shada to fight for some time in there alone so she, and by extension he, could look through his former collection of books. She ignored him, wanting to get off the island as soon as possible.

Her clothes were folded on the desk, the same ones she had been wearing when she'd jumped from the tram into the water, and before she put them on she smelled them to see if the scent of the bay was still present. To her surprise, they smelled like industrial cleaning supplies. She was grateful to shed her gown and got naked without warning the guards or waiting for them to leave.

Wearing her laundered clothes, Shada was led up the elevator and to the surface of the island. As they passed through the chain-link fence surrounding the exercise area, the dog lifted its head and watched her leave with sad eyes. It seemed this animal was used to disappointment and decided to take it without wasting the energy to stand up. As Shada was escorted to the tram, she remembered Chloe's backpack and wondered what had happened to it. She assumed the gun was lost, sitting somewhere in the bottom of the bay, but what had happened to the rest of the stuff? Shada didn't even know what was in the bag but wouldn't mind having it so she could keep something that had once belonged to her friend.

Her two escorts, bred to be muscle and not to think, wouldn't understand why she wanted the bag if she asked where it was, and she didn't feel like explaining herself. They could have taken her to someone who knew, but that would delay her departure, and she felt like she should take advantage of her opportunity to leave the island before her situation changed.

The three of them walked through the food court in the atrium at the center of the island and descended onto the platform below. Shada felt a mounting concern about the humans who had attacked her the last time she was in the city. She had no idea how much time had passed while she was on the island, though once she'd woken up, she'd felt like it was a few days at most. So the group Tony and Gustavo had held back would be gone, but what if she ran into others who wanted revenge for the edits they'd received to make them angry and impulsive, edits Ruby had blamed on Shada? She would have to keep her head down until she could get in contact with members of the resistance. They would be able to help, once they knew she was back. And when she talked to them again, how would she suggest they go along with Ruby's plan and receive the edited minds? She was lost in thoughts of their future interaction while she watched the guards on the platform disappear as the tram pulled away.

Luck was on her side when she walked through the terminal in the heart of the city on her way to board another train bound for Chloe's old apartment, to where Sikya had been left behind. Not a single person paid her any attention. If they had, and had their thoughts on revenge, she wouldn't have known, because she was too busy trying to organize her experience on the island without leaving room for the two edited minds inside her to surface.

Shada struggled to keep feelings of guilt from surfacing while she walked the few blocks between the train station and Chloe's old apartment. She had been responsible for her friend's death, but it was with the ultimate goal of saving lives. She reminded herself that edited lives were worth just as much as unedited ones; since Chloe disagreed, she had to be stopped. She was pulled back to reality and made aware of the conclusion of her trip when she heard movement behind the closed door of Chloe's apartment. The rustling stopped when she knocked on the door.

"Who is it?" Sikya called out.

"Shada."

The door opened with a rush, and Sikya stood there staring at her sister, breathing hard and pregnant.

CHAPTER EIGHT

SHADA STARED at Sikya's swollen stomach in disbelief. The last time they had seen each other, when Shada and Chloe had departed together for the island, there hadn't been any men in Sikya's life, as far as Shada was aware. "When did this happen?" she said.

"About six months ago," Sikya said, patting her stomach with a smile. Her face showed signs of the weight gain, the fullness of her cheeks framing her glistening eyes. Her black hair was pulled back in a ponytail. She was shorter than Shada by half a head, but they were built the same. Anyone who saw them could tell right away they were sisters. Sikya rushed forward and embraced her sister. "Where in the hell have you been?" she said.

"On the island," Shada said. She felt her sister's stomach press against the top of her hips. It dawned on her how much time must have passed before she had been allowed to wake up. The room might not even have been built when she was pulled from the water, and Ruby could have ordered the padded room's construction after Shada was in her possession.

Sikya pulled back and held Shada at arm's length. "We thought you were dead," she said.

"Who's we?" Shada said. She looked into the apartment, looking for the man who had impregnated her sister.

"Tony. We sort of became a thing." Sikya stepped back and put an arm on the edge of the door, inviting Shada to enter.

"Is he here now?" Shada asked as she stepped inside. The numerous plants Chloe had cared for were still thriving throughout the space, on the walls and most available surfaces. She couldn't elaborate what quality about the apartment suggested two people lived there—it could have been the way the pillows and covers were scattered on the bed or the coffee mugs on the edge of the sink, something she couldn't remember her sister doing—but she could tell Sikya didn't live there alone. Or if she did, Tony was there often.

"He's at work," Sikya said.

The sisters sat on the edge of the bed, and Shada launched into an account of where she'd been since she left her sister behind. She told Sikya how Tony and Gustavo had stayed behind on the platform to fight off the people who were coming for Shada, how Chloe had died on the train, and how she had woken up days before trapped in a padded room.

Sikya listened while Shada talked, waiting for Shada to finish before sharing her story. "When Tony got here, he said the group of people stopped fighting once the tram pulled away," Sikya said. "His face was bruised, and his arm had to be kept in a sling for a few days. He came back here to check on me, and that night was the first time he spent the night. A few weeks later, I found out I was pregnant."

Shada digested the information, calculating how long it had been since she'd left with Chloe.

Sikya told Shada she'd been gone for seven months. She left space for Shada to respond but was met with a fog of silence.

"I'm going to put some hot water on, do you want some tea?" she said, getting up by leaning to the side and using more arms than legs in order to accommodate her stomach.

"Sure," Shada said.

Sikya asked if Shada knew how Chloe had died when she sat back down.

"She took poison before her second uploaded mind, and I threw away the antidote," Shada responded.

"It wasn't them?" Sikya said, referring to the inhabitants of the island, the employees of WestCorp. "It was you?"

"She never made it to the island. I couldn't let her. She wanted to eliminate them all and make a new world ruled by the unedited." Shada waited for her sister to chastise her, but the words never came. Shada continued, "She couldn't see that what she wanted was the exact same thing Ruby wanted, to get rid of an entire group of other people just because they were born under different circumstances."

As Sikya nodded, the kettle on the stove began to whistle. She got up, made two cups of tea, and sat back down after handing Shada her cup. The chamomile-infused steam surrounded the pair.

"They're people too, and they deserve the chance to live," Sikya said with a softness bred by the prospect of bringing another life into the world. "And so you rode the train onto the island and that's where they captured you and held you the past seven months?"

"No, I used the gun Chloe had brought to shoot the window and jump into the bay. I thought I could swim back to the city, but one of WestCorp's boats picked me up. The last thing I remember before waking up was being tranquilized on the bottom of the boat."

"They kept you unconscious," Sikya said, horrified.

Shada told Sikya about the edited woman that had been

45

uploaded into her. "Marnie was put into a coma and woke up when her mind was transplanted into my body. I bet they kept me in a coma too," Shada said. A surge of anger welled up, and she paused to take a series of ten calming breaths before Hollis or Marnie could capitalize on her reactive state and take over any part of her body.

"Marnie?" Sikya said.

The awareness of the older woman inside Shada perked up, but she never tried to take any action through Shada's body.

"Marnie is the second mind I uploaded. She's in here now," Shada said, tapping her skull. "Ruby wanted to get rid of her because she spoke out against the negative edits."

Sikya took a sip of tea. "You shouldn't have accepted another one. Look how much has happened after you accepted Hollis's proposal!" She shook her head. "I swear you don't want to learn your lesson."

"I didn't have a choice! Ruby said it was how I had to earn my freedom."

"I don't trust that woman one bit," Sikya snarled, her protective instincts coming to the forefront.

"Well, I shouldn't have either, because she added another stipulation before she let me go: I have to bring other unedited members of the city to the island to accept more of the edited minds she no longer wants on her island."

Sikya set her mug on the floor and stood up with a fair bit of effort. "You have to do what? Why would you ever agree to that?"

"She said she would create more of the vengeful humans that came after me."

"So? We dealt with them once, we could've dealt with them again! We could've gone into hiding again, or left the city altogether."

"And go where? There's no hope outside the city; no food,

no water. And no city will accept us without documentation, which I'm sure Ruby can make sure we wouldn't get."

"Still, we could have tried!"

"She wasn't going to have them come for me this time," Shada said, looking at the ground. Her words were heavy, and she had trouble looking at her sister while she spoke. "She was going to have them come for you."

Sikya's eyes grew wide and her face flushed red. "I'd love to see them try! Tony would never let anything happen to me. To us," she said, her hands on her protruding stomach.

"Well, nothing's happened yet," Shada said. "This is the first place I came after the island. But I don't think it's such a bad idea."

Sikya's jaw dropped.

Shada continued. "I would teach whoever receives the upload to control the mind, and they'd then have an entire lifetime of knowledge and experiences of WestCorp. This could be the chance for peace! Ruby wouldn't want to stir up trouble because of all the inside knowledge we would have of her company."

"You two are a lot alike, you know that?"

Shada glowered at her sister. "Go on," she said.

"Both of you play with people's minds like they don't matter. What if they kill themselves, like Richard? Or worse, what if they don't and are forced to suffer through the rest of their existence trapped inside their own body, like some sort of sick purgatory?"

Shada lowered her voice. "I'll teach them how to make sure that doesn't happen."

"And what makes you so special?" Sikya said, tearing up. "How do you know it's even possible to do what you are suggesting?"

"I taught Chloe."

"Before you killed her," Sikya said.

Shada set her own mug on the floor and folded her hands in her lap. "She took the poison herself."

"But you destroyed the antidote."

"You don't agree with what I did? You want her to get rid of all edited people? You don't think they deserve the chance to live?"

"You know I don't think that, Shada!" Sikya began to sob and collapsed onto the floor. She cried until all her tears were used up. She looked at her sister and apologized. "I'm sorry I get worked up so fast," she said.

Shada shook her head. "It's fine."

Sikya stared at Shada. "I'm scared," she said.

"Scared? Of what? I told you, I won't let Ruby come for you. That's why I need to bring people to the island."

"I'm scared for Tony," Sikya continued. "And Gustavo. And the rest of the resistance. Because I know they are the ones you are going to ask to accept the edited minds."

CHAPTER NINE

Tony drove through an industrial part of the city and turned into a large parking lot behind a row of clean white warehouses. Some bay doors had cars parked outside, and some had tractor trailers backed up to loading docks. Although there was no movement outside, Shada had the sense that if the large doors were pulled up, or the trucks pulled away, each space held a flurry of activity within. The sense of stagnation and rust Shada had expected when Tony informed her they were going to this part of the city was replaced by a pleasant sense of surprise at the unexpected modernity.

Sikya was in the passenger seat, and Shada rode in the back. They had been alone in the apartment for a few hours, catching up on what had happened while Shada was on the island, when Tony walked through the door. He'd crossed the studio apartment in a few long strides and embraced Shada, grateful she had returned. She'd told Tony where she had been in the previous months and informed him about the need to keep Sikya safe by finding unedited people willing to upload edited minds. Over dinner that night, Tony had told the sisters to stay in Chloe's old apartment and that he would stay at his own place. This was

49

how Shada found out they weren't living together full time, but that Tony was there enough to walk in without knocking.

Shada stared at the ceiling for a long time during her first night in the apartment, in a bed shared with Sikya, sleepless while thinking about Chloe. Shada had spent the night next to her friend before they had gone to the island to receive the edits, before they had been offered the chance to accept the uploaded mind of an edited island inhabitant. And now her friend was gone. Shada's guilt subsided sometime in the middle of the night and she was able to get a few hours of sleep, and in the subsequent nights, she was able to fall asleep before her sister, comforted by the safety she felt being with her once more.

After a few days stuck inside, with food brought by Tony—a similar situation to when the two sisters had lived in the safe house while Ruby hunted Shada—Tony informed Shada the resistance was going to meet to hear Shada's plan. They left the next day. He had tried to leave Sikya behind in the apartment, but she refused, saying she wasn't going to let the two of them make plans that would affect her without being present.

Tony parked the car outside the warehouse at the end of the row, the empty spaces blocked from view by an all-black trailer parked in front of the loading dock next door, and the three of them got out, climbed up the metal stairs, and went inside. Shada expected to walk into a massive space but instead found a small room, an office space with thin carpet and bare drywall painted white. There was a wooden door opposite the entrance. Something about the way the sound reverberated in the room made Shada believe the room they were in was a small section inside a much larger space.

The three of them were the first ones to arrive. Chairs were arranged along three of the walls; the wall between the two doors was left bare. Sikya took a seat in a far corner of the room and sat down with a sigh, leaning back to allow plenty of space for her stomach. Tony told Shada to sit down as well, gesturing to the seat next to Sikya.

Gustavo was the next person to arrive. His black hair was longer than Shada remembered. When they saw each other, Gustavo crossed the room as Shada stood up, and he gave her a hug. More people arrived, and fifteen minutes later, with most of the seats occupied, Tony announced everyone was present. By Shada's count, there were twelve people, not counting herself and her sister. There were people of all types, from clean-cut white men to dark-haired women with tattoos and piercings, which reminded Shada of Chloe. Tony stood in front of the bare wall and thanked them all for being there.

"We haven't met since Chloe was here. I'm sure you've all heard by now, but Chloe is no longer with us." He paused, giving space for anyone to react. "She died on the way to the island."

Hollis laughed inside Shada's head before telling Shada it was her fault. She tried to ignore him but couldn't stop the guilt from bubbling up. She began counting her breaths, with the intention of taking ten. When she got to seven, she began feeling better, but Tony's mention of her name disrupted her focus.

"Shada was the first person to capture a mind," Tony said.

The entire group turned to look at her. One man, older and sporting neck tattoos, had hungry eyes that sized her up with more primal thoughts in mind.

"It was Hollis, the founder and former leader of WestCorp," Tony added.

Shada didn't know he was going to divulge this information, and she was left stunned. She shook the feeling, figuring if she was going to be asking these people to upload a mind into their own bodies, it didn't matter if they knew her secret.

"She's here now because she needs our help," Tony said.

"Shada, do you want to come up and let everyone know what you've got in mind?"

Shada had never enjoyed public speaking. Silencing her reservations, she stood up and joined Tony up front. She ignored the stares of the man who looked at her like a piece of meat and instead focused on the rest of the group.

"We have an opportunity for peace," she began. She then went on to describe how Ruby wanted to get rid of seven people from the island, and that these seven minds would need to be uploaded into seven of those present.

"Why doesn't she just kill them?" asked a shorter woman who had the sides of her head shaved.

"I asked her the same thing. She said she wants to know if it's possible to repeat the procedure Chloe and I went through, to upload a mind into an unedited body. They want to develop the technology."

"So you expect us to help WestCorp carry out their research?" the man with the hungry eyes said. He leaned back in his chair and crossed his arms.

"In exchange for the knowledge and experiences of their employees, yes. Think about it: if we know what life is like on the island, which is possible with the memories of the uploaded minds, then we would be better informed if we ever wanted to take the fight to them."

Tony cleared his throat, and everyone looked at him. "We all want to get rid of WestCorp, that's why we're here. If the upload works, why wouldn't we just use the knowledge to bring them down from the inside?"

The group nodded their heads and murmured their agreement.

"It's an option," Shada said. "I'm suggesting we use the acquired knowledge to shape WestCorp's future projects only after we agree to them. It might be a more effective strategy. What luck have you had trying to get rid of them?"

The group bristled, not used to their methods being called into question.

In the back of the room, Sikya raised her hand.

"What's the real reason you want these minds captured?" Sikya said.

Shada knew Sikya was referring to Ruby's threat to let edited humans loose in the city and blame Sikya, but she also felt Sikya was too trusting of what motivated the group. She sighed. "The minds Ruby wants us to capture are the ones who advocated for the negative edits in the first place, making the humans who came after me." She wanted to call upon their desire to help the unedited, not require their allegiance to her sister.

Shada knew this was a lie, one that Ruby had provided, since Ruby was the one responsible for the negative edits. It pained her to see the look of disappointment on her sister's face.

The lie turned out to be the spark that lit the group on fire. It started with one member of the group, a young white man with a military bearing, who stood up and proclaimed nobody deserved to be edited in the first place, let alone edited to be worse. "I'll accept a mind," he said.

One by one the group stood up, each of them saying they'd be willing to travel to the island and receive the upload. All except the man with the neck tattoos who seemed to desire Shada. He stayed with his arms crossed, his skeptical eyes darting to each member in turn.

"Doesn't anyone remember what happened to Richard?" he said. "He was taken to the island and accepted a mind too. Where is he now? Dead."

"That's different," Tony said.

"How so?" the man shot back.

"Chloe's the one who taught Richard how to control the mind," Shada said.

"Didn't she learn from you?"

"She did. But it's different coming from me."

The man squeezed his lips together and frowned.

"You don't have to agree, just don't stand in our way," Gustavo said.

The two men stared each other down until the seated one seemed to realize he was the lone dissenter. "Oh, what does it matter," he said, uncrossing his arms and pushing against the chair to stand up.

Tony told Shada to choose.

Shada first decided on Tony and Gustavo, with an apologetic look towards Sikya. She then chose four women, wondering for herself if women were more predisposed to accepting the upload of another mind, before making the young man who'd first stood up her final selection.

Tony adjourned the meeting when she sat back down. "The rest of you can leave," he said. Everyone that hadn't been selected filed out, and the man who had been staring at Shada didn't give her a second glance.

Everyone who remained looked at Shada. "When should we start training?" Tony said.

"Close your eyes," Shada told the room. They all obeyed. "Now count ten breaths."

The room was silent except for the sounds of rhythmic exhalation. When they were done, they opened their eyes, awaiting further instruction.

"Do that as many times as you can during the course of the day. We'll meet again tomorrow, and I'll walk you through the steps."

CHAPTER TEN

SHADA STOOD in front of the seven members of the resistance who would be going to the island. They were seated in two wooden church pews, four in one and three in the other, the rest of the church empty. The group had been ushered in by a young priest, or priest-in-training, who couldn't have been more than thirty. When she entered, Shada couldn't look away from a depiction of Christ on the cross, blood dripping down his face from the crown of thorns. She had been to church before, when she was young, but never when it was empty. The rest of the group strode in and sat down without so much as a second glance at the altar.

"I'm going to assume you practiced counting your breaths," Shada began. The group nodded, and she began pacing left to right, gathering her thoughts.

"So. The procedure will take place with you lying on one table and whoever is being uploaded on the other," she said. "You put a helmet on your head, Alfie or whoever is in charge will count you down, and the next instant you'll be plunged into darkness."

The woman with the sides of her head shaved blinked twice.

"The closest thing I can use to describe what it's like is being at the bottom of a well. None of your senses are available in this darkness, and it can feel like you'll be there forever. Trust me, you won't. Look for the light at the top of the well. It will be faint, like a star you can sense is there that disappears when you look right at it. Use the periphery of your sight to keep track of the light, don't focus on it."

"I thought you said we won't be able to see," the military man said.

"You can't at first, but this light will show up. It's the window back to your senses. You won't have access to your sight until you allow the light to take over your field of vision. Now, if you can keep the circle of light in your awareness, it will grow larger. This is when it's most important to not focus on it, just let it grow. I believe this is the step Choe and I were able to get through, which made us successful, and what Richard had trouble with."

Tony's and Gustavo's eyes fell at the mention of Richard's name. He had been the leader of their trio, the guy the mayor had called when he needed to protect Shada, and his loss still stung the two men.

"Now, assuming you can allow the light to grow, you'll be able to see the world through your own eyes. Then you can focus on the objects outside, until the darkness disappears altogether. When this happens, you should be able to hear the world as well."

Hollis and Marnie, their minds trapped inside Shada's head, marveled at the clarity of Shada's process. Marnie in particular wondered why she didn't have to go through this step to experience the world outside Shada. Shada informed her that she'd allowed her access so they could communicate.

"Chloe likened it to floating up from your feet to your head, and if you tried to force it, you'd fall back down."

Shada could tell this analogy resonated with the woman with long dark hair and deep-set eyes.

"This is where the breathing comes into play. It's one thing to witness the world, another to control your body. Nobody pays attention to the automatic process, so this is where it's easiest to gain access. Keep trying to find your breath until you can control each one. The person uploaded into your body won't know or register your presence."

"Is this when we take back over?" Gustavo asked.

"You could, but not yet. I tried to take over then, and Hollis was able to resist."

"And how long does all this take?" Tony said.

"Depends on the person. Now, I can do it in an instant, but the first time could take a few days."

There was a noticeable shift in the seriousness of the group. The thought of being out of control of their own bodies didn't sit well.

"The icing on the cake, what will allow you to take back control once and for all, is a serum developed by Alfie. I'm sure he'll administer it, but I don't know how soon. It's a modified form of LSD, and it allows you to sense your heartbeat."

A thin black woman raised her hand and began to speak before she was acknowledged. "This is getting weird," she said.

"Trust me, it's even weirder to go through it. But once you find your heartbeat, you can follow its resonance to every limb in your body. Keeping track of this is what will give you back full control." Shada scanned the group, waiting to see if anyone had any questions or comments. When nobody did, she continued. "To summarize, observe but don't try to force yourself back into the light and it will come to you, find your breath, then find your heartbeat and follow it to the rest of your limbs."

The process still didn't sit well with the black woman. "Sounds very . . . transcendental," she said, as if a transcendental process couldn't be trusted.

"Have you ever taken LSD before?" Shada asked.

"No," she replied. The rest of the group shook their heads as well.

"Well, it can be unsettling. But remember, it's unsettling for the person who is in charge of your body as well."

The woman with the side of her head shaved asked how Alfie would know the right time to administer the drug.

"He won't. If I had to guess, he'll give it to you soon after the upload. Or at least I'll tell him to. Don't try to skip steps though; this is the process that worked for me and Chloe."

The group all agreed, but Shada knew it was a lot for them to digest, made even more unpalatable because they were accustomed to and trained for action; the process Shada described required an acceptance of stillness.

Tony checked the time and stood up. "I think this is a good start. We should get going."

"This isn't a start, this is the whole process," Shada replied.

"That's it?" the black woman said.

"If we can do this, we'll be able to take back control of our own bodies?" the military man said.

"This is the worst-case scenario too," Shada said. "If they don't even try to keep control, there's a chance you won't have to do a thing. Be careful though: if you don't lay the groundwork, the uploaded mind could surprise you and take back control when you least expect it. That's what happened to Chloe," Shada said. The edited mind in Chloe had managed to get the word out that Shada had captured Hollis, which led to Shada being hunted by Ruby in the first place.

Tony stood and walked sideways along the pew, past the three pairs of legs between him and the aisle. Gustavo stood up and joined him. "We've got to go," Tony said. "The mayor's waiting for us."

The other five members of the resistance all looked at Shada, curious as to her business with Mayor Tensen. With her parting words, she told the group they would go over the process again, but in the meantime they should be thinking about the steps they needed to take before heading to the island. Then she left the church with Tony and Gustavo.

Mayor Tensen had reached out to Tony about seeing Shada. The trip to his new office—new for Shada, as he had been in his current position for the better part of a year—took twenty minutes from the church, since both locations were still downtown. The three of them walked past the building's security on the bottom level, rode the elevator up to the fortieth floor of the high-rise, then had to pass through another guard station in order to get to the mayor's corner office. It had a wide view overlooking the bay and, in the distance, WestCorp's island.

The mayor stood up from behind his mahogany desk and came around to greet Shada with a hug, as if they were old friends. She wasn't sure how to feel about his newfound familiarity. He then shook the hands of Tony and Gustavo.

"How have you been?" Tensen asked.

Shada, wary, told him she'd been fine. "Just getting used to being back after losing a few months," she said.

Tensen laughed but didn't seem surprised, as if it was an inside joke the two of them shared. How much did he know about WestCorp holding her hostage? It occurred to Shada to approach the authorities about WestCorp instead of getting revenge in her own way. Something about Tensen held her tongue, as if she suspected he would never be her ally. Even if she did somehow convince Tensen to go after WestCorp— which was a stretch, since the company was the reason his city was even relevant—she wasn't sure enough action could be taken before Ruby took action against a pregnant Sikya.

With all this in mind, Shada waited to see what Tensen would say. The mayor walked back around his desk, sat down, and gestured for Shada to sit across from him.

"I wanted to bring you in here today to talk about peace between the city and WestCorp," he said.

Shada was right; asking for Tensen's help would have been a waste of time.

He went on to describe how it would be best for everyone involved if they moved on from Shada's capture and imprisonment, that they should leave it in the past. "I've arranged for you and Sikya to live in one of the city's houses for visiting diplomats, a gated five-bedroom house. I can arrange for these two to be paid to protect you and Sikya." He used his chin to gesture to Tony and Gustavo. "All you need to do is leave WestCorp alone."

Shada stared at the mayor. He smiled, but she didn't return the gesture.

"Think about it," he said. "Chloe tried to take them down once, no reason for you to make the same mistake." The mayor leaned back in his chair, folded his hands across his stomach, and adopted a pastoral air. "Speaking of Chloe, how did she die?"

"She poisoned herself," Shada said. She left out her own involvement.

A look of shock crept over Tensen's face. "I'm sorry to hear that," he said. His response seemed genuine. He took a moment to absorb the news before clapping his hands together once and leaning forward. "So, what do you think about my offer? Leave WestCorp alone in exchange for the house? Live there as long as you'd like."

Shada thought for a moment. Her first instinct was to tell

Tensen she would think about it, then let the decision drag on long enough until a suitable path became clear.

Hollis had been listening and offered an alternative. "Lie. Take the house and tell him you'll be there in a few days. That way, all the people who accept the edited minds can live under one roof, with you there in case they need your help. He doesn't need to know about your business on the island."

Shada asked Hollis why he was helping her.

"I'm helping Ruby. This guy doesn't know anything about the arrangement between you two, so don't tell him. Just accept the house and get out of here."

Shada looked at Tensen. "Sounds reasonable to me," she said. She wasn't aware Tensen had been worried until she saw his face relax with relief.

"Perfect! I'll make sure Tony receives the access codes by the end of the day."

CHAPTER ELEVEN

THE TRAM STOPPED beneath the center of the island. The seven members of the resistance stood and waited for Shada to lead the way. She walked at the head of the group and tried to reconcile her decision to go back into the lion's den when the last time she'd been here she had lost months of her life.

There had been some pushback from Tony about Shada accompanying them on the trip. He said the seven of them should go by themselves, since they were the ones about to receive the uploads, and there was no need for Shada to put herself in harm's way.

Shada countered by telling them she was the one tasked with bringing them to the island. What she didn't tell him was that if they showed up without her introduction, she worried the scientists might try to perform edits to make the members of the resistance angrier and more impulsive. The last thing she wanted to deal with was a well-trained security force let loose on the city with revenge against Sikya on their minds.

The two WestCorp guards stationed at the foot of the stairs at the end of the platform stood to their full height when they saw the group disembark, each of them a full head taller than any of the visitors. Their eyes narrowed as they scanned for threats. Each one gave Shada a small nod of recognition before subjecting her to a cursory pat-down. They told the seven resistance members to place all firearms into a small bin. When nobody stepped forward to deposit their weapons, since Shada had told them to leave their weapons behind in the city, the guards began searching each person, their large hands groping men and women alike. Satisfied nobody was armed, they let everyone pass.

Shada led the group up the wide staircase and into the atrium above the platform. They emerged in the center of a food court, with edited humans walking and seated throughout, eating everything from noodles to burgers. It was clear none of the first-time island visitors expected such a modern, communal space, and their eyes scanned the room as they took it all in. Shada, who had come to the island on the tram numerous times before, remembered the first time she'd arrived and her disbelief at the comforts the edited were provided. She led her group to a rectangular table large enough to fit everyone and told them to sit down, that she'd be back in a moment.

A woman approached Shada from the direction of the information desk. "I've told Alfie you're here," the woman said.

Shada hid her surprise, but it took a second for her to understand how the WestCorp employee knew who she was there to see. There were cameras on the tram, and when she had first come to the island, the onboard computer had asked the purpose for her visit. She hadn't been questioned again, but she assumed it was because her face was recognized; now it seemed whoever she'd had the most interaction with was also notified of her arrival. As she walked back to her group of unedited, she wondered how interconnected the island was, if somehow the system knew she was tasked with bringing more people to the island so when they showed up on the tram with her there was no need to ask for their purpose. Could the cameras and microphones be recording it all, creating a vast database of every interaction on the island in order to ensure its smooth operation? It could be how Ruby knew about Marnie's conversation with her protégé.

Shada asked Hollis why the tram's computer hadn't asked why she was coming to the island with seven people from the city, and he told her it already knew the reason.

"Did Ruby tell it to expect me and seven new people?" she asked him with her thoughts. She pulled a chair from beneath the table and sat down on the same side as the three men, across from the four women.

"Didn't have to. It's always listening."

Shada wondered how much data the island had acquired about her, and how much she had produced. With a clear enough picture, could it guess what she would do next?

"That's the goal," Hollis replied.

Shada kicked herself for not closing off her personal thoughts from the mind trapped inside her.

"What are we waiting for?" Gustavo asked. His eyes were locked on the burger restaurant.

"Not sure, but Alfie knows we're here."

"Is this food specially made for the edited? Like, we could eat it too, right?" he said.

"We can eat it too. This is where everyone on the island comes to eat. It's their cafeteria."

"That's amazing," said the woman with the sides of her head shaved.

The edited humans in the food court couldn't be bothered with the newcomers. They went about their business, focused on their own tasks. Each unedited member of the resistance studied the island's inhabitants, trying to understand their enemy. Shada knew the people presented just like everyone in the city, that her cohort was wasting their time trying to distinguish a difference.

They didn't have to wait long for Alfie to show up. He had on his white lab coat, its bottom edges fluttering around his knees as he walked. He smiled when his eyes met Shada's.

"Welcome to WestCorp!" he told the group, sounding more cheerful than Shada had ever seen him.

The group muttered their greetings.

Shada went around the group and introduced each one to Alfie.

"Tony, Gustavo, and Mark," she said, pointing to the three men in turn.

"Vick," said the woman with the sides of her head shaved. "Kren," said the thin black woman. "Ophelia," said the woman with deep-set eyes. "And Sophie," said an Asian woman with short, jet-black hair.

Alfie laughed. "Pleasure to meet everyone. Did anyone want to get something to eat before we get started?"

Shada found his welcoming manner unsettling. To her relief, everyone, even Gustavo, said they weren't interested in a meal at the moment.

"Right this way then!" Alfie said.

Alfie led them down the long corridor to the lab. They passed by the decorative artwork attributed to children of increasing ages Shada had seen on her first trip to the island. She wondered where all these children were kept because she hadn't seen a single one during her time on the island. A fear gripped her: What if they were all sequestered away in a manner similar to how she had been kept in the padded room? Their edits would keep them happy, even as they grew up to become a contributing member of the island community, never knowing their treatment was abhorrent.

Shada asked Marnie where the children were, not wanting

to deal with Hollis's potentially cavalier attitude towards children in captivity.

"They're on the far corner of the island," Marnie said.

Shada asked if they were allowed to go outside.

"Of course," Marnie said with a laugh. "Why wouldn't they be?"

Shada chuckled to herself and shook her head, drawing a few quizzical stares from Gustavo. He seemed to always be aware of where she was and took steps to be near her.

Alfie led everyone into a conference room in the lab building and told them all to take a seat. "I'm going to assume Shada told you why you're here," he said.

The group all nodded.

He then explained that there would be a one-hour hijack, a test to make sure they could take back control. "Then, we'll proceed with the full upload."

The group of unedited humans looked at Shada. When she didn't offer any objection, neither did they. Seven scientists, all wearing white lab coats, then walked in and led each of the seven members of the resistance out of the room.

"They'll be back," Alfie said when he was alone with Shada. "Why don't we take a walk?" He sounded more cheerful than she had heard him before.

That ended the moment they walked outside.

"They seem nice," he said, as serious as Shada had ever seen him.

"They are."

He didn't seem in a rush to get his thoughts out. It was as if he wanted to take the full hour and not leave too much time at the end, preferring to start in silence than end in it.

The pair made a full lap around the building. When they got back to their origin point, they turned and walked around in the opposite direction. On the back side of the building, at the direct middle of the wall, Alfie spoke again.

"Don't trust Ruby," he said, his eyes still forward.

If it hadn't been so silent, Shada wouldn't have been sure the scientist had spoken.

"I don't," Shada said. She took a page from Alfie's book and didn't turn her head either. She pushed both Hollis and Marnie into the darkness, shutting off their ability to experience the outside world.

"Whatever angle you think she's taking, expect it to change. I don't even think she knows what she's doing until it's done. That erratic nature makes it tricky to come up with a plan."

"Be ready for anything, got it," Shada said.

"And now that she won't have anyone speaking out against her, who knows what she'll be able to get away with."

Shada didn't respond.

They turned two more corners than went back inside. Within fifteen minutes, the rest of the group had rejoined them in the conference room.

Alfie sat at the head of the large table and reviewed the reports supplied by his team of scientists. While viewing each one, he nodded, pursed his lips, and furrowed his brow. Shada thought he might see something that worried him even though her own inspection of the group's current demeanor led her to believe all hijacks had been successful. When she realized he'd responded the same way for every candidate, she attributed his gestures to signs of approval. Once the last file had been inspected, he arranged them in a stack, held them up, and used the table to line up their edges.

"Everything looks good to go!" Alfie said. "Now, let's get these minds uploaded."

CHAPTER TWELVE

"WHO WANTS A BEER?" Gustavo called out from the kitchen.

"I'll take one," Mark, the member of the resistance who looked like he came straight from the military, yelled back.

"Me too," Vick called out. The sides of her head were still short but she would need to get a haircut soon if she wanted to maintain her hairstyle.

"Do you all want one?" Tony said, addressing the group. They were in the living room of the house Mayor Tensen had provided, spread out on the two white couches, two white chairs, with Ophelia seated on the floor next to the fireplace. "Well, I know you don't," he said to Sikya.

Sikya pretended to be angry with the father of her unborn child. "You mean I *can't*," she said before telling him she was fine for the time being. "I might get some water later."

The rest of the group who received the uploads all nodded. Everyone but Shada. She didn't drink, not wanting it to affect her ability to control the two minds uploaded into her. She had her reservations about the ability of everyone else to maintain control of the uploaded minds while under the influence of alcohol but a single celebratory beer wouldn't hurt. If they tried to keep drinking she'd have to speak out.

"Bring out seven," Tony yelled, assuming Shada would be drinking one as well.

Gustavo brought the drinks out in two trips, setting them on the coffee table between the couches. Tony took it upon himself to hand them out. Shada shook her head when he held out the bottle brought for her. "I'm fine," she said.

Confusion on Tony's face gave way to recognition. He informed the rest of the group that they would be limited to a single alcoholic drink. "Just to be safe," he said.

"I've got this guy under control," Gustavo said, tapping his head with his index finger. "Nothing to worry about!" He laughed while trying to get Shada's attention.

Shada averted his gaze.

Tony was insistent. "No reason to put ourselves in a situation that could affect our success," he said.

Gustavo didn't push back again.

The group had taken a tour of the house when they first arrived. They looked through the five rooms and discussed who would be sharing. Tony and Sikya took a room, Gustavo and Mark another, the four women split two rooms, and Shada was left with her own. The decision to give Shada her own space wasn't ever discussed, and nobody questioned the decision. Each room had a single bed and Shada wondered if the bed would be shared or if one member of the room would be sleeping on the floor.

In addition to the five bedrooms, there was a kitchen with an island counter that could seat five on barstools, a dining room with a dark brown table large enough to seat fourteen beneath a crystal chandelier, and a study with a dark brown desk that matched the dining room table. The study had a bookshelf that was barren save for a few books left behind, paperback thrillers that could have also been left behind in a beach house.

In the basement was a small theater that could seat eight and a room with a pool table and bar. After Gustavo handed out the beers he suggested they head downstairs. "Lets get a game of pool going," he said. "We can play doubles. Shada, want to be my partner?"

Shada agreed, then Gustavo asked who wanted to be their first victim. Ophelia raised her hand and looked at Sophie, asking with her eyes if the woman would be her partner. Sophie declined, saying she was terrible at the game. "Vick?" Ophelia ventured.

Vick shrugged. "Why not?" she said.

Everyone went to the basement. While the two pairs played pool the other five lingered at the bar, with Sikya seated on one of the two barstools. Shada and Gustavo won the first game, and the team of Tony and Kren beat them on the next. Mark and Sikya said they had no interest in playing, and Sophie made no indication her mind had changed about partaking in the fun. The three teams kept a cycle of games going, with the winner staying on each time, and no team was able to string together more than three wins in a row. Everyone switched to drinking soda since there was plenty in stock for mixers, although Gustavo mentioned the various types of liquor and seemed to hope someone else would push for a shot or two. His comment was ignored.

The people not playing pool discussed their experiences with the upload. They had spent almost a week on the island, able to leave after five days. Each person had taken back control of their body by the end of the second day, a fact which inspired pride in Shada about the effectiveness of her method. The biggest issue members of the group had was her description of the light from the bottom of a well, which some of the group said was more confusing than helpful. Kren in particular said she made a breakthrough when she focused on the light instead of keeping it in her periphery.

"I'm just glad you were able to find what works for you," Shada said when she found out.

Everyone agreed that finding their breath gave them hope in their ability to take back control and that the uploaded mind never sensed their presence when they found it. The consensus was that it was a hack to keep themselves from getting lost in their thoughts, and it set them up well for when Alfie administered the serum. Within hours of the dose, each member of the group was back in full control of their bodies. No edited minds had tried to move the host's limbs since.

Shada was concerned about the uploads being completed without any resistance. Of course, Marnie hadn't tried to control any of her limbs, and Fisher hadn't tried to control Chloe, according to Alfie, but the fact that all seven uploads went off without a hitch made Shada uneasy. Her time on the island was spent in one of the dorm rooms for visitors, a barren space with just a small bed, wooden desk and wooden chair. There were numerous discussions with Alfie, the most memorable being when they discussed what uploading multiple minds into Shada might look like.

"I'd imagine you'd have to spend a lot of energy just to control them," Alfie ventured.

"Or, since there were so many vying for an increased presence, they could cancel each other out."

They were outside, walking along a gravel path between the building where she was staying and the lab where the members of the resistance were learning to suppress the edited minds uploaded into them. Alfie never said there was a chance their conversation would be recorded indoors, and Shada never pressed the issue, but whenever the two of them spoke inside

Alfie had a different air about him, an energetic disposition Shada didn't experience on their walks.

"I wish I had another body to keep the uploads in," Shada had said. She was feeling guilty about bringing the group of unedited to the island. "Like a container I alone could open."

"That would be a massive hard drive," Alfie said, his voice trailing off.

"You mean if we kept the minds on a computer?" she said.

Alfie ignored her response. "I don't even know how I would begin to figure this out, but you may be on to something. I'll have to talk to the guys underground."

She asked Hollis who the guys underground were and he told her that's what people called the employees who worked in the server room.

Alfie ended their conversation telling her he would let her know if he came up with something. "With any luck, we won't need to map one brain onto another, we can keep the blueprint in storage until it's contents need to be viewed."

Shada didn't understand. "What do you mean?" she said.

Alfie lifted both hands, balled up into fists. "Right now we map one brain onto another, using the host brain as a sort of template. Like carving a statue from a block of stone. But what if there's no stone? We would have to print it, layer by layer, until we got the complete statue."

"When you first explained the uploading process to me you said your ultimate goal was to design a mind from scratch, like an artificial intelligence. Isn't this the same?" Shada asked.

"This isn't a design, it's a recreation. Building the artificial intelligence would be like building a large block of stone, layer by layer, and figuring out what we wanted our stature to look like afterwards. Massive computational power that could be taught to perform however we wanted. This is like building a pre-existing statue instead, no teaching necessary. But much more complex."

Alfie's gaze clouded over, lost in thought. Shada tried to get him to elaborate but he didn't offer more information about his idea. When they got to the seven members of the resistance they found they had all taken back control of their bodies. From then on Shada was busy making sure everyone was taking steps to maintain a hold on their bodies, staying present in reality. She hadn't gotten time to talk to Alfie again.

Back in the basement, Shada heard her name called out. "Shada," Sikya said again. The rest of the group was looking at her when she came out of her memory.

"I think it's time to go to bed," Shada said. "For me, at least," she added, aware she wasn't in charge of the rest of the group. Though she did ask them not to drink. Even thought they had all come to an understanding, she thought it was best to say it out loud.

"We should all go to bed too," Tony said.

The group took a second to clean up before everyone went to their respective rooms. Shada put on a pair of athletic shorts and a t-shirt before climbing into bed. The sheets were softer than any she had slept in and the pillow was the perfect hardness. She fell asleep in no time.

In the middle of the night she was shaken awake by her sister. "Shada, get up," Sikya said.

Shada sat up with a big breath and looked around, alert and heart racing. "What's wrong," she said. She was upset at herself for not hearing the door to her room open, feeling like it was a lack of vigilance on her part.

"Come downstairs."

Tony was in the kitchen with Gustavo and Ophelia. In the middle of the night her eyes seemed even more sunken than before. Her defeated posture didn't help.

"I stayed awake to keep watch," Tony said. "And found her sleepwalking."

Gustavo walked forward with an open laptop in his hand. "She wasn't sleepwalking, she was using this to access a secure communication channel," he explained.

Shada's stomach dropped.

"I stopped her before she could send the message," Tony said.

Sikya alternated between looking at Gustavo and Tony. "Who was she calling?" she said.

Shada answered her sister, not needing the two men to tell her what was going on. "WestCorp."

CHAPTER THIRTEEN

OPHELIA RESTED her elbows on her knees and hung her head. "I don't remember anything," she muttered.

Tony and Gustavo looked at Shada. She wondered when she'd become the de facto leader of the group. Although Tony had made the call on his own to stay awake, keeping an eye out for threats, once he'd stopped Ophelia, it seemed his role in the matter was finished.

Shada studied Ophelia. Something made her believe the woman, but the fact remained she had tried to call WestCorp to report their location, as discovered by Gustavo.

"Check with the edited mind, see what they say," Shada told her.

"He said he doesn't remember."

Shada thought it was interesting that Ophelia also had a male mind uploaded into her body, just like she did. "Well, there's no way neither of you remembers. Someone was in control of your body."

Ophelia's eyes filled with tears. "I swear it wasn't me. I went to bed, just like everyone else, and the next thing I knew I was sitting in this chair, being shaken awake by Tony."

"I believe you," Shada said.

Sikya couldn't hide the surprise on her face. "You think the edited mind took over her body while she was asleep?" she asked.

Shada heard Hollis laugh. "Can't put anything past Ruby," he said.

"We all got control of our bodies back before we left the island," Tony said, thinking out loud. He turned to Shada. "Did you think it would take longer?"

Shada leaned against the counter across from Ophelia and crossed her arms. "No, I didn't. But I assumed the uploaded minds were weaker than the one that went into Richard, or that my ability to teach you to take back control was more effective than Chloe's." She paused. "I think they might have been planted. Or at least this mind was," she said to the room.

The five of them fell silent, a silence that was absorbed into the noiseless house in the middle of the night.

"Ophelia," said Shada.

Ophelia lifted her head and stared at Shada with bloodshot eyes.

"Don't ask if they took over. Go in and find out yourself."

Ophelia nodded, closed her eyes, and took a series of long breaths. She looked peaceful, like she was deep in meditation, but Shada knew how hard it was to access the memories of an uploaded mind for the first time. While Ophelia searched, Sikya met Shada's gaze. Shada closed her eyes and nodded, instructing her sister to be patient. It was a full eight minutes before Ophelia opened her eyes again.

"He was told by Ruby to allow me to take back control at first, then wait until we were settled before trying to contact the island."

"It's just like with Chloe," Shada muttered.

Tony and Gustavo shot Shada an inquisitive look, but she

didn't elaborate. She asked the two men to look into the memories of the minds uploaded into their bodies as well, to see if there was a similar conversation with Ruby buried in the archives.

After minutes of silence, both men reported the minds inside them had been tasked with infiltrating the resistance.

"Ruby didn't share her ultimate plan," Gustavo said.

"Mine says he thinks Ruby wants to eliminate the resistance. He was told to wait until he'd witnessed the entire group together before attempting contact."

"Ophelia was confirming the edited minds made it to the city," Sikya ventured.

Shada cursed herself for not looking into the identities of the minds before they were uploaded. She assumed they were all like Marnie, older and waiting for their natural expiration, and had spoken out against Ruby, drawing her wrath. She never considered they were working for Ruby, with Ruby, to take down the unedited resistance from the inside. Hadn't Alfie told her not to trust Ruby? His words of advice echoed in her mind.

Tony tasked Gustavo with waking up the rest of the team and told Sikya to go back to bed. She protested until Shada told her there was nothing she could do. "This could take a while," she said. "I'll let you know what happens."

When the entire group was in the kitchen, Shada asked them to all dive into the memories of their uploaded minds to find out if they had been instructed to offer little resistance to the host's attempts to take back control. "Find out if the minds inside you are planning to establish contact with WestCorp in the future."

All eyes fell on Ophelia as they realized this was why she was the first one in the room, and why she was so upset.

"Why wouldn't we have found this out before?" Vick asked Shada.

"You didn't know what questions to ask. It's like an encyclopedia. Lots of information, but if you don't know where to look, impossible to know it all."

The team fell silent as they searched the memories stored inside them. It took some longer than others, and Shada had to kneel in front of Mark and guide him through the breath work before he was able to access the memories of the mind uploaded inside him. In the end, all the team members reported the edited were in fact sent by Ruby and told to allow the team to take back control with minimal resistance after the initial upload.

"Ruby wanted it to be a surprise when they took back over," Sophie said.

"We need to find out who we're dealing with," Shada declared. She told the group to find out the former identities of the minds that were uploaded into them and write down their previous roles in WestCorp. "In particular, find out how old they were," she said. Based on her experience with retired West-Corp members, Shada guessed they were easier to control and posed less threat.

The group all closed their eyes. Kren was the first to break the silence. "They don't know their age because their birthday wasn't celebrated."

Shada thought for a moment. "See if they spent time in the dream station before uploading." She knew from Hollis that the only people who used the artificial sleep machine were the ones with nothing to do, that the productive members of the island were expected to work and therefore didn't have the time to spend in another reality.

All the team members said the edited minds hadn't used the device, that this was the first time they'd experienced anything outside of their own bodies.

Shada's stomach dropped when she considered the possibility that Ruby might have selected her strongest supporters on the island. "Find out their opinions of the unedited, in particular how they feel about nonstandard, post-birth edits."

The group dove back into the archives of the edited minds. One at a time, their eyes opened, and they each sat in silence until the last member of the group came back to the room. Vick was the first to speak. "This one doesn't care about what kind of edits WestCorp provides, she trusts Ruby's judgment."

The other six nodded in agreement, each discovering the same sentiment.

A wave of guilt crashed over Shada. She'd been betrayed by Ruby and had led the members of the resistance, including the father of her sister's baby, into a trap.

"What should we do?" Gustavo asked.

Tony spoke up before Shada could say anything. "We need to make sure nobody can contact the island. We'll sleep in shifts, a group of three and a group of four. If we limit ourselves to six hours a night, it should be manageable."

"Not ideal though. Less sleep means there will be more time awake, draining mental energy," Shada said.

"But also less time for the edited mind to take back over," Tony countered.

"From now on, everyone needs to remember the uploaded mind allowed you to take back control. Imagine a scenario when you'd need to fight back, and practice the breath work with that added focus," Gustavo said.

"Should we take the serum?" Tony asked. Alfie had sent the group back with a considerable stockpile, but Shada had told them not to use it since they had been able to maintain control over themselves without it. She herself didn't use it and had imagined the group was at the same level as her. Now she wasn't so sure.

"Yes, take the serum and begin your training all over again, with the knowledge that the minds inside you are lying in wait," Shada said.

"And what if the minds inside have heard this entire conversation? They'll know what we're trying to do," Vick asked.

"Practice accordingly," Shada responded.

"Will we have to keep this up forever? Afraid to sleep out of fear they will take over, always waiting for them to show up?" Kren said.

Shada sighed. "For now, yes."

Kren's eyes narrowed. "What do you mean, for now?"

Shada told them about her conversation with Alfie, about their idea to create an external server for uploaded minds. "The edited minds could be stored in there, leaving you alone again."

"They would live forever," Vick said.

A look of disgust swept over Sophie's face. "Why should they get to be immortal? Shouldn't we be able to upload too?"

"In theory, you could upload when you die, if you wanted."

Everyone in the group fell silent.

"What would be the point of uploading and living in a computer?" Mark said.

"Could I upload into someone else?" Gustavo ventured.

"I'm not cursing someone else with this," Mark said.

"You know what would be nice? If we could upload into a blank human. Or swap with them," said Vick.

"Where are you going to find a blank human?" Sophie shot back.

"You'd have better luck uploading into a robot," said Kren.

Something in Shada clicked, and she realized the group might be on to something. "They're called androids," she said.

CHAPTER FOURTEEN

NOBODY LEFT the house for the first few days after Ophelia's nighttime attempt to contact WestCorp. Their groceries were delivered, and teams of two took turns cooking for the group, with Tony joining Sikya and Shada in a group of three. There wasn't a strict schedule or assignment of who cooked the meals; a loose volunteer system emerged where everyone contributed. The group spent each evening in the basement, some watching a movie and the rest in the pool room, even if they weren't playing. Mark turned out to be the best player of the group, and nobody was surprised to learn there had been a table in his childhood home.

Four days after the discovery of Ruby's plan, Tony and Gustavo left to meet with the rest of the resistance. They told the group beforehand there was a chance their identities would be discovered by WestCorp, if they weren't able to block the edited minds inside them from witnessing the meeting, but that extra precautions would be taken when they slept to prevent communication with the island. None of the resistance chose to skip the meeting, but it was conducted in a public place so their warehouse location would remain secret.

Ophelia moped around the house. Everyone tried, in their own way, to cheer her up, but she couldn't recover from the guilt of putting the group at risk. She never played pool, just sat and watched in silence, and when she watched movies, she had a far-off look in her eyes, as if she could see the screen but wasn't processing the story. Shada wondered if Ophelia would be able to take action in the event of a threat, but Tony assured her Ophelia's demeanor wouldn't interfere with her work.

A week after Tony stopped Ophelia from sending a message to the island, Shada received an unexpected one. Alfie contacted her by sending the message to Tensen, who relayed it to Tony, who delivered it to her.

FOUND COMPUTER ENGINEER. COME TO ISLAND WHEN READY.

"Tensen called me and asked what the computer engineer was for, said he thought you agreed to stay away from West-Corp. I told him I'd get back to him after I talked to you," Tony said.

Shada was surprised Alfie had followed through with their discussion. She was still interested in the storage device but never imagined it had landed on the scientist's list of priorities. His message left her with more questions than answers. Had the computer engineer already solved the storage problem? Did Alfie want her to come to the island to test if she could upload one of the minds inside her into the device? Or did Alfie want her to upload the engineer, joining Hollis and Marnie, so he could work on the problem while inside her mind?

She told Tony to tell Tensen the truth. "Tell him we're making an advanced storage device," Shada said.

"He'll be able to guess it's for the uploaded minds," Tony said, who guessed its purpose as well. He closed his eyes and took a deep breath, followed by a slow exhale, before opening his eyes again. The members of the group all adopted Shada's attitude about the minds uploaded into their bodies: pretend they don't exist.

"Even if he guesses, what can he do?" Shada asked.

"He could tell Ruby, if she doesn't already know. WestCorp contributes so much money to the city that Tensen does everything he can to keep her happy," Tony said with disgust. As a member of a group that proclaimed itself to be for unedited rights, it had to be tough to know his boss was in bed with the enemy.

"I'll worry about her when the time comes." The leader of WestCorp was a sore subject with Shada after her lies about the edited minds that the group had uploaded.

"Are you going to go back to the island?" Tony asked.

"That's the plan."

Sikya approached Shada about the message from Alfie that evening. Shada didn't wonder how her sister found out; she assumed Tony would tell her and had braced herself for the conversation.

"Another upload?" Sikya said. They were alone in Shada's bedroom. Shada had just finished a session of breath work when her sister knocked on the door and asked to come in.

"All the message said was he found a computer engineer. How do you know they're going to be uploaded?" Shada asked. She herself wasn't sure what Alfie had in mind.

Sikya tilted her head and stared at her sister. "Because I know you. If the project was going to be completed in the real world, Alfie could have taken care of it himself and wouldn't need you to go back."

Shada squeezed her lips together and nodded. "Alfie and I never discussed uploading another mind. If the engineer was uploaded, how could they test their work? I think the message meant that he'd found someone to work on the problem, and that I can come back to the island because it's been solved."

"What problem is that?"

"How to store uploaded minds outside a body."

Sikya's jaw dropped. "If it works, could we clear everyone here, get them back to the way they were?" Tears welled up in her eyes, and she wiped them away with her fingertips.

Shada was sure her sister missed the way Tony used to be. "In theory."

"Would you upload Hollis, and what's her name, into the device?"

"Marnie," Shada said. She hadn't given any thought to clearing the uploaded minds from her own body, but now that the potential had been vocalized, she knew she would keep them. They had become a part of her, a part she didn't want to get rid of. "I don't think so. I've got a firm hold on them, and they weren't sent to lie in wait for my defenses to drop. I've known from day one what they can do and haven't had any problems yet."

"Then why go to the island at all?" Sikya asked.

"He could want me to test the device. If it works, we can send the others. They deserve to sleep in peace."

"You should consider leaving those two inside the device as well," Sikya said, her chin pointing to Shada's head, her word choice not matching her rabid tone.

Shada knew her sister wanted her to get rid of the uploaded minds, but if Sikya used strong language, Shada would double down on her decision to keep them. "I'll consider it," Shada said, a lie, since her decision was already made.

"What happens if Alfie does want you to upload the engineer and you lose control with him in there? Have you considered that?"

Shada laughed. "It hasn't been an issue yet," she said. "Hollis was the most difficult, for me and perhaps anyone. Compared to him, Marnie was a breeze. Even if the engineer gets inside and wants to take over, Hollis will put up a fight. I think—and I could be wrong—that the more minds uploaded, the less of a chance any one of them takes over. If anything, I would present like a person with multiple personality disorder, each identity coming to the forefront for a period of time before they lose control to the next."

Sikya tilted her head back and stared at the ceiling in frustration.

"And that's the worst-case scenario. Odds are I keep control of them and nobody notices a thing." Shada waited until her sister looked at her, then met her gaze. "Trust me, I'll be fine."

Sikya looked away. "There's no reason to keep poking West-Corp. We should get Tensen to help, trust the authorities. If they knew what WestCorp was doing, they would be shut down."

"Ask Tony how he feels about Tensen," Shada said, knowing the doubt he held about the mayor's loyalties. "I met with Tensen. He knew they took me hostage and he asked me to let it go! You really think the city has the power to stop WestCorp? WestCorp owns the city. The money they provide is the only way the city sustains itself. Tensen knows that."

"But he's on our side," Sikya said, referring to those who fought for the advancement of unedited rights.

"Was on our side. When money wasn't involved. I don't trust him."

Their conversation was interrupted by Gustavo knocking on the doorframe. "You two should come downstairs, you'll want to see this."

The sisters exchanged a curious glance before leaving the room. When they got downstairs, they found everyone crowded around a laptop, with the news playing onscreen. Ruby was front and center. The leader of WestCorp was at a podium addressing the media. Shada recognized the island in the background.

"What's this about?" Sikya asked.

Gustavo informed her that Ruby was offering free post-birth edits beginning the next day. The banner at the bottom displayed the information in text.

"This isn't good," Tony said. Some of the group nodded in agreement, and some ignored Tony and kept their eyes on the screen, their jaws clenched, shaking their heads in anger.

Ruby's announcement bothered Shada. There was a scratchiness inside her that wouldn't go away. What did the woman want? The last time free edits had been provided, the resistance had to protect Shada from vengeful recipients of the procedure. Shada wondered if these edits were of the same variety, that the people subjected to the change would be told the members of the resistance were responsible and would hunt them down.

"Sounds like something Ruby would do," Hollis said. "Since she hasn't heard from any member of the group."

For a split second, Shada wondered if they should have allowed Ophelia's attempted communication to succeed but altered the message she sent.

"Too late, what's done is done," Marnie said.

Shada agreed. No point in second-guessing the group's decision. She knew one thing for certain: if the storage device did exist, they needed to use it. The members of the resistance would be needed and couldn't be expected to stay locked away in a house, afraid to sleep.

"I've got to get to the island," she told the group. Everyone turned to her and stared.

CHAPTER FIFTEEN

SHADA'S DESIRE TO go back to the island came as a shock to them all.

Gustavo looked as if he had been betrayed. "Wait, you want to get edited?" he said.

Tony hadn't told anyone but Sikya about the message from Alfie, so Shada filled everyone else in. "I believe he's found a way to store a mind outside the body. I need to find out for sure, so we can store the minds you've all uploaded onto the device."

Ophelia's face brightened for the first time since her uploaded mind's attempted betrayal of the group, a spark of hope lighting up her darkened eyes. Vick and Kren both looked at their feet. Sophie was shocked.

"What if we want to keep it?" Sophie asked.

"That's your choice," Shada said. "I would never force you to do anything."

"If you're the only one, you'll have to find a way to sleep without putting the rest of us at risk," Gustavo said.

Sophie grew defensive. "And what if I don't?"

"If you don't, then why would we let you stick around?" Gustavo shot back.

"That's not up to you to decide. The group would have to make that decision," Mark said. "If she wants to keep her uploaded mind, I'll keep mine as well, and we can help each other."

The two of them looked at each other, and Shada wondered if they were harboring a secret romance.

It was decided that Tony would accompany Shada on her trip. She wanted to go by herself but was told it was too risky. Mark thought Shada shouldn't go at all, that two of the team members should go talk to Alfie instead.

"The message was for me," Shada said. "There's a chance the storage device isn't even done, that he needs me to help finish the project."

"What would he need you for?" Vick said. "If you could have solved the problem, you wouldn't need the computer engineer."

"If the engineer needs to be uploaded, who better than her to accept another mind?" Sikya said. Her attitude towards Shada's trip had changed the moment it was decided Tony would join her, and Shada knew she wanted Tony back the way he was before. He would be able to sleep without worry, and Sikya would still be safe because they had fulfilled their end of the bargain.

"Agreed. If the message was for Shada, then she has to go," Tony said. "We'll be back as soon as possible."

Nobody pushed back again.

Tony and Shada left within the hour. Ruby's announcement had come in the early evening, and it was already dark by the time the pair left the house. Shada had been stuck inside for days, and being outside again felt like leaving her protective bubble. They decided to take the train into the heart of the city, where they would then catch the tram to the island, so the vehicles could be left at the house in case they were needed by those left behind.

Shada was surprised at how many people were walking towards the train station with them. Not many people lived in that part of the city—since the houses were so large and expensive, not many could afford to live there—but the few who did were streaming from their residences, with more joining as they went.

"Ruby said the edits won't be offered until tomorrow," Tony said.

"Maybe they're lining up," replied Shada.

The underground train station was full when they arrived. There was one attendant, since normal travel volume at that time didn't require more, and she was busy helping people get their tickets and pass through the turnstiles. When Shada and Tony got onto the platform, they were met by a sea of people waiting for the next train to arrive. A display said it would be there in eleven minutes.

"There's no other reason all these people would be out at this time," Tony said. "Everyone's going to the island."

"I can't believe everyone wants to be edited," Shada said, looking around. "I wonder if Ruby's expecting this kind of volume." She hoped the edits Ruby was providing were the standard type, to make everyone happier, healthier, and smarter. If not, if Ruby was going to edit them to be angry and impulsive, the people still at the house would soon be in danger.

Shada remembered those who'd blamed her for their not receiving the standard edits. They had hunted her down and almost got their hands on her before her trip back to the island with Chloe. Did any of them still roam the streets? Could they be here, on the platform with her? She hoped they'd learned their lesson from their first experience with WestCorp and were staying far away.

Tony must have sensed her fear, because he shuffled closer to her, his eyes scanning for threats.

They boarded the train together when it arrived. Every seat was taken, and the remaining passengers had to stand squeezed together in order for everyone to fit. The passengers were silent.

Shada studied the people packed in the train with her. Her heart sank when she saw children, some still in pajamas. She hoped their parents weren't taking them to the island and told herself they were on the train for some other reason, any other reason, like going to the hospital because they were sick.

"Stop lying to yourself," Shada heard Hollis say. "Those kids will be edited alongside their parents."

Shada closed her eyes and counted ten breaths instead of engaging with the edited mind inside her. She hoped the children would get off every time the train stopped at a different station. They never did. Each platform they stopped at was filled with people, and since nobody disembarked, their car wasn't able to accept more passengers. The closer someone was to the heart of the city, the longer they would have to wait, if they wanted to take the train. Of course, they could always walk, and Shada had a feeling these people would get to the tram any way they could.

The entire contents of the train spilled onto the platform when it pulled to a stop beneath the heart of the city. Shada looked inside the train before it pulled away and saw a solitary older woman, homeless by the look of her and the amount of luggage she had. She must not have heard about the free edits, and Shada imagined how confused she was after being joined on her trip by so many people before being left to continue on alone.

There was a line to get to the lower level where the tram that would take them to WestCorp departed. It stretched up the stairs and went out the entrance. She wished she had a special pass, one that said she had business on the island and wasn't there for the edits, but who would look at it? She remembered the information desk at the end of WestCorp's tram platform. It was worth a shot. "Come with me," she told Tony.

WestCorp employees were on the platform maintaining order, distinguishable by their smiling faces, khaki pants, and white polos. There were queues where each of the tram doors opened, and unedited inhabitants of the city stood five deep in each. Shada asked a WestCorp employee if she could get to the island sooner since she wasn't going for the edits.

"Sorry, everyone has to wait in line," a smiling man with salt-and-pepper hair told her.

"What about those who need to commute to the island tomorrow morning?" she asked.

"All meetings have been rescheduled."

"What if I'm edited and need to get back?"

The man's smile broadened, showing off straight white teeth without imperfections. "All edited were told to stay on the island or risk being left in the city. These people are our first priority," he said with a wave of his hand.

An older unedited woman, in her late sixties or early seventies, smiled at what was taken for superior customer service.

Shada shook her head and began walking the length of the line. The gates were kept open as the line stretched through them, and Shada asked a station employee if they were still ticketing. "No ma'am, WestCorp paid to keep these open."

The line stretched down the city blocks approaching the station. Tony and Shada took their place at the end as more people stood behind them. She had never seen a line so long and wondered how long it would take to move to the front.

Hours went by. At first, they had moved a few steps every fifteen minutes, but towards the middle of the night their progress stalled and never began again. She thought people would leave the line, but those around her sat down on the sidewalk instead, not willing to lose their spot. Close to dawn, word reached them that there was a one-in, one-out policy, since the island was full, meaning that one tram car would depart for the island as soon as a full one arrived.

The line moved again as the sun rose. Everyone knew this meant the first edited people were coming back to the city, and all eyes turned towards the station. Sirens rang out within minutes of the line making progress, and emergency vehicles raced towards the entrance to the station.

"What's going on?" everyone seemed to ask at the same time.

Word trickled back that there were people upset with waiting so long they'd begun vandalizing the area around the entrance, hoping to scare away those waiting in line. Shada's heart sank at her suspicion that the destruction was committed by those just returning from the island.

Twice more the line moved forward, meaning two more trams had returned. Shada and Tony were now three blocks from the station's entrance and could see a line of cops, in full riot gear, who had set up on the far side of the street.

The sound of glass breaking rang out in the early morning hours, followed by an explosion. Shada stepped into the street and could see flames on the far side of the station. Nobody abandoned their spot in line, convinced the damage was done with the sole purpose of scaring them to do so.

Shada watched as the cops scattered and began trying to apprehend those in front of the station who were rioting. One young man evaded them and ran down the street towards her. Tony pulled her back into line and placed himself between her and the street.

As the young man approached, Shada saw his ecstatic eyes

and was shaken by the grin on his face. He seemed to enjoy being chased. The cops behind him yelled for him to stop.

The young man reached in his pocket, pulled something out, then slammed it into his arm. He threw it to the side, where it landed on the ground next to Tony.

It was a clear, finger-sized vial, with WESTCORP written in black on the side.

"So they used my idea," Hollis said.

"Guess so," Shada thought in reply, staring at the vial that had been full of Stim moments before.

CHAPTER SIXTEEN

SHADA EXPLAINED to Tony what the vial had contained. "It keeps you wired. They gave it to me when I was on the island so I wouldn't sleep. I've never had so much energy in my life."

Tony turned back from watching the police's pursuit of the young man. "You think they gave the stuff to everyone coming back from the island?" he said.

"It wouldn't surprise me. All that extra energy would have to be burned somehow, that's why they are vandalizing the city. It's only going to get worse as more people return."

The line marched forward and stopped half a block closer to the entrance. "I think we should go back," Tony said.

Shada cocked her head. "Why? Once we get onto the island, you can get the edited mind out of you. You'll be back to normal."

"Assuming that the storage device is even finished. You don't know that for sure."

Shada nodded, agreeing that Tony presented a fair point.

"Plus, what if Ruby told them to hunt us down, like she did for you? We're sitting ducks out here," Tony said. He kept leaning into the street and looking towards the station, monitoring the destruction from afar.

Thick black smoke rose in the distance. Tony told Shada a car up ahead was burning.

"We need to get out of here," he said again.

"Now that we're making progress? Come on, we've already been waiting all night."

"The closer we get to the station, the larger the chance one of them spots us."

"Assuming Ruby told them to go after us," Shada said.

The line moved forward again. They were now two blocks away. Shada leaned into the street as well and watched another batch of people with fresh edits stream from the station. There were dozens of them, and after taking one look at the scattered police officers and the destruction caused by those who came before, they ran in every direction, looking for something to destroy themselves. It was as if they'd walked into the city and were unleashed to join in the fun.

One pair, a man and a woman, left the fresh destruction behind and ran down the street in the direction of Shada and Tony. Tony stepped out into the street when they got close.

"Hey!" he called out to them, getting their attention.

The two individuals stopped in their tracks. Their heads tilted to the side and they blinked twice, as if they were animals in the wild who had just spotted their prey. They leaned forward and walked towards Tony, crouched, ready to pounce. Tony pulled out his pistol.

"What did I tell you?" Tony called over his shoulder.

Inside Shada's head, Hollis laughed. "Shouldn't have stopped that girl from contacting WestCorp," he said.

Marnie responded. "Don't distract her. You do know if she gets killed, we do too, right?"

Shada closed her eyes, took a deep breath, and blocked both minds from communicating with her.

With a curse, Shada stepped out of line and stood next to Tony. At the sight of Shada, the woman stood up straight, turned around, and yelled in the direction of the station entrance. "Over here!" she said.

One new arrival heard her, and when he saw two of his fellow edited being held at gunpoint, he turned around and yelled for more of the edited to follow him. Five more, farther away, heard his call, and instead of continuing to break windows where they were, they began walking towards Shada and Tony.

"Agree we've got to get out of here?" Tony said.

"Agreed."

Tony walked backwards, his gun still on the approaching pair, and Shada did the same. They were waiting for the opportunity to run. The edited man who'd communicated to the other five jogged forward until he was with them. The three of them could rush at any moment.

The gun went off before any of them could make their move. One of the men collapsed in a heap, writhing on the ground and holding his leg. A second shot rang out, and the second man fell as well. Both had been shot in the leg.

The woman with them didn't bother to inspect if they were all right. She lunged forward, sprinting at Tony and Shada as fast as she could. Tony fired a third time and the woman collapsed in a heap, clutching her side. The five edited in the distance began sprinting.

"Run!" Tony said.

Shada sprinted away as fast as she could. Tony, behind her, instructed her to turn right down a side street, through the line that stretched off into the distance. They ran for a block then turned left. Shada continued for as long as she could down the street parallel to the one they had stood on the entire night before she slowed to a walk and turned to see if they were still being pursued.

All five new arrivals turned the corner, running as fast as they could, the taller, thinner ones in front, the slower ones behind.

"Could use some of that Stim right about now," Tony said through heavy breaths.

"We'd never stop running," Shada replied.

Tony told Shada to go into an apartment building. The entire city seemed to be shut down, its inhabitants all waiting in line for their free edits. Soon, they'd be joining the pursuit for Tony and Shada as well.

Inside the apartment building, Tony and Shada found the staircase and began climbing. They were on the third floor by the time they heard footsteps below. On the fifth floor, Tony told Shada to exit the staircase.

"We've got to find somewhere to hide," he said. Shada could tell Tony was focused on keeping control over his breathing, scared the mind inside him would use the danger as an opportunity to take back control of his body. When Shada tried the door of the first apartment inside the hallway, Tony told her to keep running until they turned a corner. "In case they look into the hallway from the stairs," he explained.

They found an unlocked apartment and rushed inside, shutting the door behind them without a noise. The air was stale, and the furniture belonged to another decade. They assumed it was empty until a weak woman's voice called out from the back. "Diego? Is that you?"

Tony followed the voice to the back bedroom. He popped his head inside and held a finger up to his lips. When Shada looked in, she saw a white-haired skeleton of a woman, so old her days couldn't involve much movement. She assumed Diego was the elder's son, or caregiver.

The woman's eyes, fearful at the sight of Tony and the gun in his hand, pleaded with Shada for protection. "What's going on?" she asked Shada. "Why does he have a gun?"

Shada knelt next to the woman's bed. "We're here to protect you," Shada said. "Diego sent us. He's on the way to get edited now."

"Diego's always so thoughtful! I'd go too, but I can't leave the apartment," the woman said, resting her head on the pillow with a sigh.

Tony and Shada spent the day with the woman. There was no sign of their edited pursuers, or Diego, but Tony kept his weapon ready. The woman had plenty of canned food. Shada and Tony ate one meal, wanting to leave as much food as possible for their host because they didn't know how long she would have to last on her own. Both of them knew if Diego was edited, he wouldn't be coming back for her, he'd be hunting for them and the rest of their group.

They decided to wait until nightfall to try to make their way back to the house Tensen had provided. They discussed the possibility Tensen would tell Ruby where the group lived, and they convinced themselves that Tensen would keep their secret safe. They hoped. Both Shada and Tony referred to the group as a whole, but each knew they both prioritized Sikya's safety.

Travel across the city was slow without the train. They took care to move between buildings so they could hide if necessary and made it more than halfway back on the first night. Their day was spent hidden in the chemical storage room of an industrial cleaning company, and their projections put them back at the diplomat's house in the middle of the second night.

Their plan didn't account for the barriers.

The first barrier they encountered was a pile of cars stacked up in the street. Bright lights accompanied by the rumble of heavy engines streaked by on the far side. A block over was another barrier, this one built from concrete dividers. It was as if the city had spent the day erecting walls to keep everyone apart, dividing itself into sections. Shada assumed it was the work of the unedited locals and not the returning edited, even though the new arrivals were the ones with Stim and could have worked the hours necessary to get the job done.

Shada and Tony were forced to travel through buildings to get past the barriers, instead of running through streets and using buildings as way stations. They managed to get past the first set of barriers by moving through a convenience store and kept looking for the vehicles they'd heard before, not knowing if they belonged to the city or the edited. Not being able to travel through the streets made their trip take much longer than expected, and they got back to the neighborhood of the safe house right after dawn. The street outside was abandoned; to limit their exposure, they approached the house from the rear, hopping between backyards.

They knocked on the back door and Kren answered.

"Where have you been?" she exclaimed when she saw them.

Within moments, everyone was at the back entrance, even those who had been asleep, grateful to see Shada and Tony alive.

When Sikya rushed forward and gave Tony a hug, Shada felt both happy her sister had found someone and sad she wasn't the first one Sikya embraced. Her place in Sikya's life had been taken. Sikya pulled away from Tony and hugged Shada.

Shada was quiet while Tony told the group how they had been standing in line when the riots began and had to come back. It didn't take long for his own questions to begin.

"Has anyone come here looking for you?" he asked.

Gustavo told him no. "We wanted to leave, to look for you, but we thought you might show up here, so we stayed put."

"Good," Tony said. "The edited are coming back to the city to hunt us down."

CHAPTER SEVENTEEN

"The reports say the unedited are rioting to scare people from getting WestCorp's free edits," Gustavo told Tony and Shada. "It's all over the news."

Tony shook his head. "The people coming back from the island were the ones rioting. They got to work as soon as they left the station."

"They've been Stimmed," Shada added. "With all that extra energy, Ruby just had to point and off they went."

"Stimmed?" Sophie asked. She twirled a pen in her fingers while she sat at the kitchen table.

"A compound WestCorp developed so their workers could push past their physical limits. No need to sleep," Shada explained. "They gave it to me when I was held hostage to keep me awake. I've never felt so energized."

Sophie nodded then stared at the pen crawling across the back of her hand.

"Tensen instituted martial law," Sikya said. She didn't bother to hide her frustration. "Accepted money and support from WestCorp to get the city back in order."

Gustavo and Tony met each other's gaze. "He's gone off the

deep end," Gustavo said. "He doesn't care about the unedited anymore, if he ever did in the first place."

"I think he did before Ruby got into his ear," Shada said. "That woman is an expert manipulator."

"He divided the city into districts: Alpha, Sigma, and Theta. Said his goal was to keep the riots contained to specific areas," Sikya said.

"We had to pass by some of the borders," Tony said. "Looks like they were made of whatever was available: piles of cars and concrete. The area around here seemed untouched, but we need to get out of here. If anyone finds out where we are—"

"Or if Tensen tells Ruby where we are," Gustavo interjected.

"We'll have some serious problems."

"Where should we go?" Kren asked.

The group fell silent while they tried to come up with a solution.

"Could we go to the warehouse?" Ophelia said.

"In theory, yes, but it would present the same challenges as here: we're trapped if they find us. Both the warehouse and here could work as long as nobody finds out where we are."

"Are you worried somebody would give up our location?" Ophelia said. "We already sleep in shifts; I don't think it would be one of us."

"It's more about the lack of exits. If we'd had time to prepare, we could have made an escape tunnel, but that's not an option now."

Gustavo suggested they take the high ground. "If we find a high-rise and stay in the upper levels, we could see everyone coming into the building. We could cut off the elevator and block the staircases."

"And if they found us all they'd have to do is wait," Vick said.

Gustavo looked down at the floor, thinking. "What if we go to Tensen? He has a ton of security, his office is high up, and if we're there, we can make sure he doesn't say anything to Ruby."

"All he'd have to do is get a single message out. That's going to be difficult to stop. His priority is the city, and WestCorp has him convinced they are helping," Tony said.

Silence descended on the group. "Instead of going up, we could go down," Shada said.

Everyone looked at Shada. Kren was the first to speak. "What do you mean?"

"The tunnels. If we need places to run, it would make sense to be in a series of tunnels. We could split up if we needed to and pick where we come back onto the surface for supplies. Not much light, and probably smells terrible, but it could work."

"The tunnels," Tony said, chewing on the thought. "It does work."

"What made you think of that?" Gustavo said with a chuckle.

"I was just thinking about escaping, how it would be nice to be near a train."

Gustavo was impressed. Shada's face flushed.

"We could enter at the train station, walk until we found somewhere to set up camp," Tony said.

"What if we don't want to go?" Vick said. Her nose was turned up.

"Then you can stay on the surface and wait to be found. The way this city is being torn apart, it's not if, it's when."

She was quick to backtrack. "I was just saying, in case someone didn't want to go."

The group decided they would wait until night to leave under the cover of darkness. Tony and Shada excused themselves and went to sleep, their first proper rest in days. Everyone else took turns sleeping in shifts in preparation for their long night, even though some of them had just woken up when Tony and Shada arrived back at the house.

Packing for the journey took place throughout the day. Everyone carried two bags when they left, one filled with their own personal items and a second with items the group would need: food, toiletries, and cookware. Everyone was responsible for as much water as they could carry. The plan was for them to travel in three groups of three and meet up at the train station, each group traveling along a different route. Shada and Sikya were placed in separate groups, since it didn't make sense for one member of the resistance to guard two of them. Tony made sure he went with Sikya, and they took Kren with them. Gustavo stayed by Shada's side during the assigning of groups, and the two of them were joined by Sophie. Ophelia, Mark, and Vick made up the third group.

Since Sikya was pregnant, they had her group take the shortest route to the station, a straight shot that avoided open road. Mark, Ophelia, and Vick left first, making an arc out to the left before turning back in the direction of the station. Shada's group's route was the mirror image, an arc to the right, and Sikya's group left last. If anyone was watching the house, the hope was they would follow the first two groups instead of going after the slow-traveling Sikya.

The trip went by in a blur. The next thing Shada knew, all nine travelers were underground, in the darkness of the tunnel between the station and the heart of the city. Vick handed out glow sticks. Everyone cracked them and used the meager light to inspect their surroundings. The tunnel was filthy, filled with a variety of paper trash, and a thick layer of grime covered the concrete walls. Sikya covered her mouth with her shirt. The light from the glow sticks didn't reach the ceiling, but it illuminated the numerous pillars, casting shadows into the dark spaces beyond.

"Let's start walking," Tony said. "If anyone hears a train, let us know so we have plenty of time to get out of the way." Pregnant women weren't known for being quick on their feet.

"The trains have stopped running," Gustavo said.

"Part of the whole martial law thing," added Kren.

"So we shouldn't hear anything. But if we do, give the rest of the group a heads-up."

Tony and Gustavo led the way, with Shada and Sikya right behind them and the rest of the group in the rear. Every so often, Tony would point to the ground without saying a word, calling Gustavo's attention to something without stopping to investigate. It took Shada a few times to realize there was evidence of other people who had traveled through the tunnel before them.

A flickering light up ahead made Tony stop the group. He told Mark and Vick to investigate while everyone else stayed back. It turned out to be a group of unedited squatters who had come down to the tunnels when the riots began. "They said to keep walking, then turn left down a side passage. There's an area where we can set up," Mark reported.

The area the group was directed to was at the intersection of three walkways. Each walkway was large enough to accommodate the tallest workers, but the intersection of the three opened up to a high ceiling. A large wall on one side was covered in graffiti. Nobody objected when Mark said, "This will work."

The group cracked open a prepared meal, the last home-cooked meal they expected to eat for a while. There wasn't any use in saving food for later since there was no way to keep the leftovers from spoiling. The men ate more than they would have under normal circumstances so the food wouldn't go to waste.

Tony, Kren, and Sophie were assigned the first watch, a person for each walkway leading into the space. They were tasked with keeping an eye out for intruders in addition to making sure none of the group woke up and tried to contact WestCorp.

From where Shada lay, she could see Tony's back as he sat in the middle of the passage that faced the wall. She had trouble falling asleep, since she had slept the entirety of the previous day, and she hadn't eaten enough food to make her eyelids heavy. She guessed an hour or so went by while she focused on her breathing. She watched as Tony turned around to inspect the group. She squinted to hide the whites of her eyes, kept her face relaxed, and witnessed Tony stand up and walk away without making a sound.

He was gone too long for a bathroom break. No, he left, then came back while everyone but Shada was fast asleep.

CHAPTER EIGHTEEN

SHADA SLEPT through the changing of the guard. When she woke up, Tony, Kren, and Sophie were fast asleep. Ophelia, Vick, and Mark were posted at the three entrances to their space. "Where's Gustavo?" she asked Sikya.

Sikya was lying on her back, her hands on her stomach. "He said he'd be back before he walked off. He's been gone for a while now," she said. She beckoned Shada over with her head and whispered, "Come here."

Shada crawled over.

Sikya took Shada's hand and placed it on her stomach. "Can you feel him?"

"It's a him? When did you find out?" Shada said. Her eyes fell as she waited for a kick.

"I just know it's a boy," Sikya whispered, as if she didn't want to scare the child inside her.

Shada felt a series of rumbles beneath her hand. She looked at her sister and smiled. "He's dancing in there!"

"Has been all morning."

They lay next to each other while the others slept. Shada debated whether or not she should tell Sikya about Tony's nighttime trip. She still hadn't decided what to do when Gustavo came back and knelt down at their feet, off the blankets, on the cold concrete floor. He looked at his watch. "They'll be awake soon. We should get some food ready."

Shada pulled out a camp stove and boiled a large pot of water. With it, they made instant oatmeal and coffee. The smell woke up the three sleepers, and once they were awake, the three who stood guard were able to leave their posts and join them.

Shada waited until everyone finished eating before she said what was on her mind. "We should find somewhere else to set up," she said.

Ophelia was collecting everyone's trash. "Why? We just got here."

Shada didn't want to share her concern that Tony had given up their location. Instead, she said it would be best if they found somewhere with more space, so they didn't have to live in such close quarters. "We could set it up so people could sleep apart from everyone else, a room with one door if we can find it. Those who are asleep wouldn't be disturbed, and one person would be enough to watch them, instead of three," she said.

"I found a group of people in a blocked-off train station half an hour's walk from here when I was out exploring," Gustavo said. "We could take a corner of the platform and find a bedroom for when some of us"—he gestured to the seven resistance members—"need to sleep."

Everyone looked at Tony. He let the suggestion digest for a moment before agreeing with the move. "Pack everything up then, we'll head out soon."

Whenever Sikya tried to help, a member of the group told her to sit back down. They'd packed light, so it didn't take long to be ready to move. Gustavo led the way down the tunnel, with the same reminder as before to keep an ear out for trains. There still wasn't a single sign that any of the trains were running.

The tunnel curved to the right. The space ahead became more illuminated as they walked, until the entrance to the station ahead could be seen, a circle of light in the distance. It reminded Shada of coming back to reality for the first time after being hijacked. She realized she hadn't heard from Hollis or Marnie for some time. Instead of checking in on them, she left them alone, content with them staying in the background.

Tony told the group to stop at the entrance to the station. "Get your eyes acclimated to the light," he instructed.

Shada got a whiff of sewage while she waited for her eyes to adjust. Hollis started complaining, so she blocked him from using her senses to experience the world. She wished it was possible for someone to do the same to her so she could escape the stench too.

There were three groups of people on the two platforms. One group was in each of the far corners, and the third group was set up in the middle, on the right side of the station. Both entrances were blocked off, one with piles of furniture and one with broken concrete rubble that had bent rebar sticking out at odd angles. A boy, no more than nine, was playing with a rubber ball on the right platform. The ball rolled in the group's direction. He chased it down and saw the nine people waiting in the shadows. His jaw fell, and he froze. Shada saw Sikya, ahead of her, flash the boy a smile. Without grabbing his ball, he turned and ran. He reached a woman in the middle of the platform— his mother, judging by her age—and buried his face in her side, clutching her around the waist. She rubbed his head. He turned to the where the group stood and pointed. His mother hurried over to a group of seated men and leaned in close to one of them.

The next thing Shada knew, four men were walking towards their location, baseball bats in hand.

"We should go out there," Gustavo said.

"Did you already meet them?" Sophie asked.

"Nope, I stayed here and watched them for a minute before coming back."

"Let's go introduce ourselves," Tony said. He led the way into the light of the station, both hands raised.

The four men stopped their approach when they saw the number, and quality, of people who showed themselves. Shada and Sikya both used their hands to shield their eyes, but the other members of the resistance strode forward, tall and proud-chested.

"Hello!" Tony said, doing his best to sound welcoming.

"Hello," said the man in front, the one who had been informed of their presence. "What can we do for you?"

Tony hopped up onto the platform and the rest of the resistance followed. Shada kneeled on one leg and offered her bent knee to Sikya to use as a step, which Sikya refused, and Ophelia reached down to help the pregnant woman climb up. She managed to get both knees onto the platform, then stood up one leg at a time. Shada was last to get onto the platform; she placed both hands on the edge and threw a leg up before standing up to join the others.

Tony waited until everyone was on the same level before kicking the boy's ball back to him. "We were wondering if we could set up camp here," he said. He looked around. "We could take that corner," he said, pointing to the end of the opposite platform. "And guard against others coming in from the tunnel."

By now, the rest of the women and children on the platform had gathered behind the group of men. A man on the far platform called out, "Everything all right over there, Jimmy?"

"Everything's fine," Jimmy, the leader of the small group, responded.

"She's pregnant," a woman who appeared to be Jimmy's wife called out.

"I see that, honey," Jimmy said.

One of the men whispered into the leader's ear. Both pairs of eyes fell to the waistbands of the resistance members, noticing their weapons for the first time.

Jimmy's face fell for an instant before he flashed Tony, and the rest of the group, a smile. "Make yourselves at home!" he said. He lowered his voice. "But take the end of the platform on this side, you don't want to set up in that far corner."

Tony thanked the man, and Gustavo oversaw the setup of their camp. Four of the group were instructed to put their belongings along the wall closest to the tunnel, and the other five were told to put their stuff along the wall closest to the entrance, the one blocked off by piles of furniture. He put the camp stove, food, and water in the corner, explaining he didn't want the other groups to see how much and what kind of food they had. "Food and water are going to be the biggest things for us to worry about," he said. "Carrying it down from the surface isn't going to be easy, for anyone."

The young boy, who was curious about the newcomers taking the space where he played with his ball, was lingering nearby. When he heard Gustavo talk about water, he said the water fountains in the middle still worked. "That's where we get our water from," he added, before chasing his ball back towards the area his family occupied.

Shada looked at the group, pretending she was seeing them for the first time. They were all thin, sinewy, and it was clear from their matching outfits and the hard looks on their faces they were not people to be messed with. With this in mind, she informed the others she would walk over to the camp and introduce herself to the neighbors alone. Just inside the edge of the middle camp, she saw the water fountain on the wall near the blocked entrance. Part of it had been removed so larger containers could be filled.

Jimmy came out to meet her. "Do you need something?" he said, his voice cold.

"Just wanted to introduce myself," Shada said. In her mind, Shada heard Hollis add, "So she can drink your water."

Jimmy stood still before the boy's mother rushed forward, scolding him. "Where are your manners?" she said. She looked at Shada. "My name is Caprice," she said, walking forward and extending a hand.

"Shada," she replied with a smile.

"I'm sure you've seen my little guy, James, running around. Just tell him to leave you alone if he bothers you."

Shada laughed. "I'll keep that in mind."

Marnie communicated to Shada through shared thoughts. "They seem nice," she observed.

Caprice gave Shada a tour of their encampment, the one in the middle of the platform. The one in the farthest corner was Caprice's sister's family. The two camps were mingled most of the time, so when Caprice was finished the first tour, she showed Shada the setup on the far end as well. There were three other men in the two camps, two women, and a couple of surly teenagers who didn't look Shada in the eye. All their names were shared, but Shada retained none other than the first family she'd had contact with.

"Across there is Tim and his family. We don't go over there."

"Any particular reason?" Shada said, doing her best to sound curious without being intrusive.

"They use the corner of the platform as their bathroom instead of going off into the tunnels. It's gross over there; best to just stay away."

A white sheet hung in the far corner. The stench near the tunnel made sense now.

"I noticed a water fountain . . ." Shada said, her voice trailing off.

"Right." Caprice paused. "We don't share it with them." She pointed across the station with her head. "But since you've got a pregnant woman with you—"

"She's my sister," Shada said.

Caprice smiled, appreciative of sisters who stuck together. "Then you guys can use it. Fill up containers for emergencies, while it still works."

"We appreciate it," Shada said. "Let me go back and let them know."

"We'll talk soon!" Caprice said as Shada walked away, sounding like they were friends who had just had lunch together.

The boy stood near the wall of the platform, halfway between his family's two camps. There was just enough room for him to play without going near the edge. He waited until he was sure Shada was paying attention to him then kicked the ball in her direction, so slow there was little risk it would fall onto the train tracks. Shada kicked it back. The boy smiled and left her alone to walk through the middle camp and back to her own.

CHAPTER NINETEEN

THERE WAS nothing for the group to do but exist once their space was organized. They had light, shelter, and water, and meals required two people, at most, to prepare. The members of the resistance performed body-weight exercises to pass the time.

The bathroom situation was the first problem to be addressed. Sikya asked Gustavo if she should share the same area in the far tunnel their neighbors used as a bathroom. Shada overheard the question and said she thought Caprice would show her where to go.

"Let's just find our own spot," Gustavo said to Shada. "I don't want us to have to walk across the platform every time we need to use the bathroom." He looked at Sikya. "Let's go into the tunnel and see if we can find a good spot."

Sikya looked uncomfortable at being joined by a man. Sophie offered to go with Sikya. "I can stay with her while you find somewhere for us to sleep," she said to Gustavo.

Gustavo agreed, since it would save a later trip. Tony helped Sikya down onto the train tracks and watched the three of them disappear into the shadows.

Shada was on edge the entire time her sister was gone. She

could tell Tony was too. When Sikya walked back into the light a half hour later, she crinkled her nose at the smell coming from the opposite platform. Both Shada and Tony helped pull her up from the tracks.

"We should build a set of stairs," Tony said, thinking out loud.

"You don't want to do this every time?" Sikya said. Her breathing was heavy.

Tony let out a relieved laugh, able to relax now that Sikya was back.

Shada took her sister by the arm and made her sit down with her back against the wall. Tony lingered around them, waiting to see if there was any way for him to help.

"If we stay here for a while, I don't know if I can keep doing that. This guy's getting bigger by the day," Sikya said. She tapped her stomach; she could have been referring to her belly or to the baby inside.

"There's a maintenance room a short walk from here where we can sleep," Gustavo reported. Everyone could hear him, since they lived in such close quarters. "Took me a while to get the door open, but it will work well."

"It took you a while because you had to wait for me," Sophie said with a smirk.

"Right, she picked the lock in no time at all. I was going to shoot it if I had to."

"And where are we supposed to go to the bathroom?" Ophelia asked.

"There's an open space just inside the tunnel. Past the pillars on one side of the track," Sophie said.

"Whoever goes has to bring someone else with them," Tony said. He looked at both Shada and Sikya. "One of us, to keep an eye out. Just in case," he said, referring to the members of the resistance.

"I can't go to the bathroom unless you hold my hand," Gustavo said. His expression didn't change.

Tony chuckled and shook his head. "Only you," he said.

Gustavo grinned and gave Shada a wink.

Gustavo and Shada turned away from the group and joined Sikya with their backs against the wall. She was watching the boy play on the far side of the middle camp.

"I wonder if this guy will play sports," Sikya said, tapping her stomach.

"I'm sure he will," Shada replied. "I'll be the one to teach him!"

Sikya looked at Shada with tears in her eyes. "Will there even be sports to play for unedited people?"

"Of course there will be!" Shada said. She wasn't as confident as she sounded, but she wanted to cheer up her sister.

"The world is changing. I don't want him to have to deal with WestCorp just to have a future," Sikya said, her voice full of sadness.

The sisters and Gustavo sat in silence. Shada was the first to break it. "I'm going to get back to the island and stop the edits," she declared. "This little guy doesn't need to grow up in a world like this."

"How are you going to do that?"

"Not sure," Shada admitted. "I'll blow up the lab if I have to."

Gustavo stared at Shada. "What about storing the minds on the device? Alfie can't do that without a lab," he said.

"Well, what's the point of getting the edited minds out of everyone if there's no city to return to?" Shada said.

Neither Gustavo nor Sikya said another word.

Marnie told Shada she should spend the night with Gustavo, and Hollis accused Marnie of having a crush on the mischievous man. "It's clear he likes her," Marnie said. "They're both young and strong. Why not?"

Shada read Hollis's thoughts and learned about his disgust at the prospect. She hadn't considered how getting physical with a man might not be something Hollis would want to witness, and she communicated, through her thoughts, that she'd block him out if it ever happened.

Marnie told Shada to leave her alone. She wouldn't mind seeing the act occur.

"Bet you wouldn't," Hollis responded.

Shada took ten controlled breaths and ignored the two bickering minds.

Over dinner that night, the group discussed how soon they would run out of food. Kren calculated they had enough for the next four days. "I think we should make groups of two or three, head to the surface at night, and see what we can gather," she said.

"Three," Tony said. "Two can carry most of the supplies and the third can protect them."

Gustavo suggested they make a trip in two days. "That way, if the first group doesn't find anything, we can take another trip before we miss a meal."

Everyone agreed. There was an awareness of Sikya and the life growing inside her that nobody vocalized. They could go hungry if necessary, but she couldn't.

Tony said they needed to decide who would keep watch over the room while the first shift slept. Tony, Kren, and Sophie had taken the first watch the previous night, and the task would fall to one of them. Tony said he would prefer to stay on the platform with Sikya, and nobody disagreed. Kren offered to watch the door while Mark, Vick, Ophelia, and Gustavo slept.

"And who's going to guard the second shift?" Tony asked, talking to the four who would sleep first.

Mark offered to do it, and nobody had any objections.

With the first shift of sleepers gone, Shada and Sikya were joined on the platform by Tony and Sophie. They both had to stay awake until it was their turn to rest. Shada tried to sleep but found the constant light distracting. She tossed and turned, and when she faced Sikya, she saw her sister was wide awake as well. They exchanged a thin-lipped smile before Shada closed her eyes and counted ten breaths.

She was woken up by a gunshot from the tunnels.

By the time Shada had opened her eyes and sat up, Tony and Sophie were already on their feet, heading towards the noise. At the end of the platform Tony stopped, leaned over as far as he could, and looked into the darkness.

"Kren!" he shouted. The name echoed off the walls in the tunnel until it was replaced by silence.

"We have to go," Sophie said.

Tony looked back at Sikya and told her he'd be back before leaving with Sophie.

More gunshots rang out soon after they disappeared into the tunnel. Shada could sense the distress her sister was under, her own nerves responding to her sister's elevated state. A few tense minutes passed before six of the group emerged from the tunnel and jumped onto the platform. Tony told Mark and Vick to cover the entrance to the station. The two of them nodded, turned around, and kept their weapons aimed at the shadows.

"Kren stayed back to cover us," Gustavo told Shada when he saw her counting those who had returned.

A series of gunshots rang out, and Shada knew, deep down inside, she would never see Kren again.

Tony helped Sikya stand while telling her, "We have to move."

Sikya stood and began gathering her things. Tony told her to leave it all. He grabbed her arm and pulled her towards the far end of the platform. Everyone from the other camps had already fled into the tunnel.

Gunshots rang out close behind them. They were near the water fountain when Sikya screamed in pain and fell to her knees. Tony knelt beside her.

Shada watched as her sister reached down between her legs, and her hand emerged covered with blood.

"Were you shot?" she asked.

"No," she said through gritted teeth. "The baby—" Her words were choked off by a groan.

Gustavo pulled on Shada's arm. "Come on, we've got to get out of here," he said.

"No! Not without her," Shada said.

Gustavo overpowered her. "Let Tony take care of her. You've got to get back to the island, remember? Nobody else can do it."

Shada struggled to get back to Sikya's side.

"It's what she would want," Gustavo yelled.

An earsplitting explosion forced everyone to look back at the tunnel. Where Shada had been lying down asleep just minutes before was now a crater. Rubble was everywhere. The mangled bodies of Mark and Vick were on the floor, their limbs at odd angles. Shada watched as WestCorp forces, identifiable by their white polos and khaki pants, streamed into the station. They all wore black body armor vests and black tactical helmets. There were at least a dozen of them.

CHAPTER TWENTY

SELF-PRESERVATION TOOK over and Shada began to run. Gustavo led the way, crouching behind the left-behind gear in the other camps as he went. The shouting and the gunshots behind them blended into one cacophonous mess of sounds.

The next thing Shada knew, she was in the tunnel with Gustavo, Sophie, and Ophelia. Tony had stayed behind. The three remaining members of the resistance took up positions behind cement pillars with their weapons aimed at the entrance to the tunnel. A WestCorp member jumped down from the platform and ran into the shadows. Three gunshots rang out, and he fell forward in a heap. Gustavo fired once more, ensuring the pursuer never stood up again.

Shada looked further into the darkness of the tunnel. The rest of the displaced platform dwellers had their eyes wide open as they watched the action unfold.

After a series of frantic gunshots on the platform, another person jumped down and began running into the tunnel with their hands up.

"Don't shoot!" Tony said. He dove into the shadows on the

dark side of the wall that separated the platform from the tunnel.

Shada rushed forward without a second thought, ignoring her own safety. "You left her behind!" she said. She punched Tony in the face, and was about to again, when he caught her hand.

Another series of gunshots rang out, and three more members of WestCorp fell to the ground just inside the shadow of the tunnel.

"Stop!" Tony said to Shada. "Listen, she told me to! She couldn't move, and she wanted me to help you get to the island," Tony said.

Shada tried to strike him with her other hand. "Why did you listen to her?"

He was about to answer when a man's voice from the platform yelled into the tunnel. "Give up the fight!" he said.

Shada froze.

"You're resisting the inevitable. We're the future, you just haven't recognized it yet. Help us save the city."

His words were met with silence. Shada knew he was talking to her, that this message was from Ruby.

"Everyone is getting edited; you can too. No questions asked. We'll forget about the men you killed."

"We won't!" Gustavo shouted.

In the dim light, Shada saw Tony shake his head in frustration at his comrade's outburst.

"If you're still listening, we don't expect you to come out. We'll take care of the pregnant one on the island; she'll be given the best care."

Shada's blood boiled at the smirk she imagined was on the man's face.

"And you can show up whenever you like to receive your edits. It's time to join the future!"

"This is all your fault," Shada whispered to Tony.

"My fault? She told me to leave her behind!"

"You shouldn't have listened to her," Shada hissed. "Where did you go when you left? You went to tell WestCorp where we were, didn't you?"

Tony was shocked at Shada's sudden accusation. "What are you talking about? I never went anywhere."

"The first night, when you stood guard. I watched you walk away."

Tony paused for a moment before closing his eyes. "I dozed off," he admitted with a sigh.

"And when you did, your implanted mind took control and walked away from the group to tell WestCorp where we were. She trusted you!" Shada hit him in the chest. "We trusted you."

Everyone else in the tunnel was silent. They could hear the retreating footsteps of the team from WestCorp as they walked away on the platform. Gustavo stepped forward, stood in the shadow of the tunnel, and reported seeing their attackers leave the station. "They've got Sikya with them," he said.

Shada didn't want to watch in case she got the urge to run through the station to try to take her sister back by herself. "We should've kept moving," she said, more to herself than to Tony.

"We hadn't even been there a night," Tony said, looking at her.

"But it was long enough for them to catch up with us!"

Tony was still grappling with the knowledge he'd put the group at risk. "I woke up in the same position as when I shut my eyes. I could have sworn it was just a second," he said, shaking his head.

"That's all it took to put us in danger."

Tony absorbed the weight of his mistake. "Did you tell the others?"

"No."

"Are you going to?"

"I might."

"Let me tell them," Tony said.

As mad as Shada was, she couldn't deny how much she respected his courage.

Their private conversation was interrupted by Gustavo telling Jimmy to wait before entering the station again. "They could have left people on the far side of the wall," he said.

"I don't care," Jimmy said. "I'm going back to get my stuff."

Gustavo looked into the shadows towards Tony and Shada. Shada wondered if he could make out any more than their outlines in the darkness. "A little help?" Gustavo said.

Tony stood up and walked into the middle of the tunnel, in front of Jimmy. "We'll make sure it's all clear." He looked at Gustavo and used his lips to point to the far wall. He and Gustavo stood on each side of the tunnel, both looking across the span at the platform beyond the far wall. They crept forward, alternating between looking onto the platform and looking at each other, with subtle head nods indicating that the platform on their comrade's side was clear. When they had inspected each corner, they gave the all clear. Gustavo waved the other groups into the station.

The bodies of three dead WestCorp attackers were left on the platform, close to where Shada had tried to sleep next to her sister minutes before. Shada looked at the spot where her sister had fallen; there was blood on the ground. Not much, but enough for her to wonder if her sister's child would make it to term. Caprice didn't let James leave her side while she inspected their camp. Tim and his cohort settled back into their space as if nothing had happened, making Shada wonder how much chaos they'd seen on the surface before descending underground.

Tony told Gustavo to help him with Mark's body and asked

Sophie and Ophelia to take Vick's, telling them he wanted to leave their bodies, along with Kren's, in the room Gustavo had found for them to sleep in. "When this is all over, we can come back and give them a proper burial," he said.

The somber survivors nodded. While Shada was alone on the platform, she couldn't shake the worry that WestCorp was waiting in the shadows for them, that the group was walking into an ambush, and she waited to hear the gunshots that would signal a second round of fighting.

To occupy herself, she began collecting all salvageable supplies, the things that had survived the blast that killed Mark and Vick. In the corner, their food and water had fallen over but was still intact. The bags that were closest to the tunnel were all damaged beyond use. She gathered their remaining supplies near the blocked-off entrance to the tunnel, arranging them into small piles on the platform floor.

A loud noise rang out from the far side of the platform. Shada jumped, thinking it was the first shot of a gunfight, before realizing the sound had come from the wrong direction. In the far camp, Caprice's sister stood up with a frying pan in her hand and a sheepish look on her face. "Sorry!" she yelled to all.

The four surviving members of the resistance emerged from the tunnel, weary and slow-moving. Their climb onto the platform seemed to take forever. Everyone assembled around the pile of gear Shada had created while they were gone.

"I've got something to tell you guys," Tony said.

Shada turned away to give the tears welling in her eyes time to reabsorb.

"It was my fault they found us," he began.

"No, don't say that. We all chose to set up camp here," Gustavo said.

"But how'd they know to look for us in the tunnels in the first place?" Sophie asked.

"Exactly," Tony said with a nod to Sophie. "They knew because I told them."

If Gustavo had been shot at that exact moment, he couldn't have looked more surprised. Ophelia's understanding eyes stayed on Tony's face, urging him to continue.

"Shada said she watched me walk away when I was supposed to be keeping watch at the first camp," Tony said. "I remember dozing off for a second, but I snapped awake right away. Or so I thought." Tears began streaming down his face. "I could've sworn it was only for a second!" He closed his eyes and wiped his cheeks with the back of his hand.

When Shada put a reassuring hand on Tony's shoulder, she heard Hollis laugh. "Guy gets your sister taken and you feel bad about a few tears . . . you unedited are too much!"

Marnie was quick to jump in. "Don't you see he already feels bad enough? She's going to need his help if she's going to get her sister back."

"He'll help get her back either way," Hollis said. "It was his mistake, he'll fix it. There's no reason to worry about making him feel better."

Shada took three deep breaths and silenced them both. She didn't care to hear either of their opinions about her actions, and for the first time she wished she wasn't under the constant scrutiny of these inner voices.

"What do we do now?" Sophie asked. Ever practical, she wanted to figure out the next step, not caring to analyze those previous. Ophelia looked like she wanted to give Tony a hug but maintained her distance, and Gustavo still looked shaken that the leader of their small group was the one who'd put them in danger.

"We have to get to the island," Shada said. Now that West-Corp had her sister, she was going back whether they went with her or not.

Tony looked at Shada and nodded. "I'm with you," he said. "Let's go get her back."

Gustavo also agreed to make the trip. "And once we get her back, we can find a way to stop the edits and save the city."

"And get these uploaded minds out of our heads and into the computer," Ophelia said. "If we want to," she added, looking at Sophie.

Sophie studied the faces of the other four members of her group. Sensing their resolve, she said she would join them too. "I don't want to miss out on the fun," she said with a smirk.

CHAPTER TWENTY-ONE

BEFORE THEIR DEPARTURE from the barricaded station, the group emptied the contents of the bags Shada had salvaged. They took stock of what had survived and repacked the available gear into four duffel bags, one per person. Since they were heading to the island instead of setting up camp again, they didn't need food, kitchen supplies, or toiletries. They made sure to pack their weapons and ammunition, even though Shada knew these items would be confiscated by security the moment they tried to step onto the island. Everyone had extra clothes, and Tony reminded them to keep a pair of socks they could change into on top, since they'd be on their feet for the foreseeable future.

Shada found Caprice and told her they were leaving. "Feel free to take everything we leave behind," she said. "There's some food left, and cookware."

Caprice thanked Shada before telling her she was sorry about what happened to her sister. "I don't know what I'd do if anything happened to mine," she said, turning to look at the other camp.

Shada didn't mention that they were on their way to get her back. All Caprice knew was that they had decided to move on.

"Best of luck," Shada told Caprice. James walked by holding his ball. "Hope he stays out of trouble."

"Everything will go back to normal once we're back on the surface," Caprice said. "We just have to wait out the storm."

Shada marveled at the woman's inability to grasp the fundamental transformation the city had undertaken. She wanted to grab Caprice by the shoulders, to shake some sense into her and convince her things would never be the same again, but she realized hope was the one thing keeping the transient wrinkles in her face from becoming permanent evidence of constant worry. "It'll pass soon enough," Shada said. She returned to her section of the platform, grabbed her bag, and nodded in the direction of the far tunnel, indicating to the group it was time for them to set out.

They walked for hours, each step taking them closer to the heart of the city and the tram that would take them to the island. There were thirteen stops between them and their destination.

Shada tried to picture how they would get onto the tram without waiting in line so they could limit their risk of exposure to the edited humans returning from the island. Was there a way they could get to the front of the line as soon as they showed up? They could hold the mass of unedited back at gunpoint, but WestCorp could stop the tram from running, leaving them in an extended standoff with a massive disadvantage in numbers.

She hoped the WestCorp employees at the tram had been told to expect her after their message had been delivered.

"See how hope can make it easier to take one step at a time?" Marnie said.

Shada was appreciative of the insight but wasn't a fan of the edited mind commenting on her thoughts.

Some of the stations they passed through were exposed to the night air, even though the tracks between them ran through underground tunnels. The half moon was in a different location in the sky each time they surfaced. The buildings on the sides of the station grew more prominent as they approached the heart of the city, over time becoming too tall for them to see more than a few stars through thin cloud cover.

They emerged from underground and walked beneath a broken bridge on their approach to one of the exposed stations, stepping over rubble from the collapsed middle. The skyscraper on their right had numerous windows overlooking the tracks. "Keep your eyes open," Gustavo said with a nod to the array of glass.

Twice, Shada thought she saw eyes following their movements. She found darkness both times she focused on their location and was left wondering if she'd imagined the feeling of being watched.

The walls of the station were covered with turquoise tiles, the most distinctive station they had passed through on their trip. The station had the same layout as the one they had been in when WestCorp attacked, with two sets of stairs in the middle of the platform, one on each side, that rose up from the station's platform to the surface above. A dog in the corner of the platform was gnawing a bone. He growled before taking his bone up the stairs to find another private location to enjoy his prize.

The group left the moonlight behind and entered the darkness of the tunnel once more. As they got closer to the heart of the city, they found more and more evidence of previous human presence: tattered rags, discarded food wrappers, and evidence of small fires. There was even an abandoned pillow and blanket.

The last station they passed through before their destination was underground. In the tunnel on the far side, they found a handful of people seated in the shadows on each side of the tracks. Shada kept her eyes ahead of her, worried they were edited and would come after her and the group, like the edited who had chased her and Tony on the surface.

Not one of them moved.

Gustavo cracked a glow stick and held it up high, searching their faces.

"Look at them," he urged the others. "They're all sick."

Shada saw unresponsive eyes set in hollow sockets. Their skin was pale, and each one of them was bent in half, clutching their stomach. Their sunken cheeks looked as if they were sucking air through straws. If it wasn't for the rising and falling of their chests, they could have been dead.

A young man pointed to a cracked pipe with a container positioned beneath to collect dripping water. "Don't drink it," he said.

Gustavo used his glow stick to look into the container before showing the rest of the group. Flecks of metal floated inside. Concerned their own water was contaminated, they withdrew their personal containers and inspected them. Each person's water was clear. Shada wondered if Caprice and her family would have to resort to drinking tainted water from an underground pipe if, or when, their water fountain got turned off. James had no chance of thriving if the storm never passed.

Tony told the rest of the group they had to keep moving, that they were close, and to ignore the people on the sides of the tracks. A short walk later, they saw the light of the station at the heart of the city. Both sides of the platform were filled with people.

The five travelers walked into the light. The people closest to the tunnel were aware of the emergence of the group but turned away after a quick glance. A sense of relief washed over Shada when she realized everyone was unedited and waiting for their chance to get to the island. They climbed onto the platform at the first possible opening in the mass of people.

The station presented an extraordinary amount of stimulation after the trip through the dark tunnel. The artificial lights were incongruous with the hour, and a new ecosystem had developed to service the long-waiting unedited. There were food vendors, small stands where books and magazines were sold, and signs for private bathrooms for which use could be purchased instead of using the facilities provided by the station. Most clusters of people were asleep, but some of the older men were gathered in a group, each clutching a small paper cup of what Shada assumed was coffee.

Shada led the group through the waiting unedited to the staircase that led down to WestCorp's private platform. People even waited on the steps, their heads resting against the wall as they rested.

The WestCorp employee closest to the stairs, one of many dotting the platform, greeted Shada and her group when they arrived. He was wide awake and smiling, average height, average weight, and had an average face punctuated by a thin beard. "Good morning!" he said to Tony, even though Shada was the one in front.

Shada wanted to punch him in the face.

"Mornin'," was Tony's gruff reply. "We need to get to the island."

"So does everyone else. Please wait in line. As soon as another group comes back, the line will start moving again."

He inspected the group, still grinning, before addressing Tony again. "Is there anything else I can do for you?"

Shada stepped between the employee and Tony. "Yes. Talk to whoever's in charge, Ruby if you have to, and get us on the next trip. We were told by one of you to come to the island."

The WestCorp employee blinked twice before requesting a

moment and walking away. At the information desk on the far side of the platform, he leaned over the counter to talk to a seated woman in private.

The unedited who were awake stared at Shada and the members of the resistance. They nudged those closest to them and used their eyes to direct attention to the five people not standing in line. Those people then nudged the people in front of them, and they repeated the sequence until the unedited who were next in line to board the tram were wide awake and staring at Shada, Tony, Gustavo, Ophelia, and Sophie.

Shada felt like she'd just walked into the lion's den. She could tell the members of the resistance were on edge as well; their eyes searched for threats, and their taut postures prepared them to spring into action at a moment's notice. Sophie made her intentions clear by resting her hand on the grip of the handgun at her side.

CHAPTER TWENTY-TWO

THE WESTCORP EMPLOYEE came back a few tense minutes later. If he noticed the stare-down between the various unedited, he didn't acknowledge it. He made a beeline for Shada and her group, with that grin still pasted on his face, and said they would be on the next trip to the island.

"That's not fair!" one of the unedited near the front of the line yelled out.

"They just got here! We've been waiting for days!" another said.

One woman, a teenager, left the line and rushed towards the WestCorp employee closest to her, a middle-aged woman. Shada couldn't hear their exact words but watched as the employee smiled then gestured with an open hand to the back of the line.

"I just came over to talk to you!" the teenager exclaimed.

"The line begins back there," the employee said, loud enough for everyone around to hear.

The line shifted as the abandoned spot was filled, like a snake moving a single coil.

The teenager pulled her arm back to strike the WestCorp

employee. Her arm then passed through open air and she lost her balance. Two male WestCorp employees came from nowhere, grabbed the teenager, and escorted her away.

Shada and the members of the resistance were taken to the front of the platform to wait for the tram to arrive. They stood with their backs against the wall, facing the horde of angry unedited. An hour passed, then two, and Shada would have fallen asleep if it wasn't for the constant threatening glances thrown their way. She assumed the rest of the group was exhausted as well after their overnight journey.

It occurred to her there was no reason for the others to stay awake. It wouldn't matter if anyone woke up under the control of the edited mind, since they were heading to the island and to Ruby. She was about to suggest they take turns resting, leaving some of the group awake to monitor the unedited surrounding them, when the tram pulled up.

The five of them were given an entire tram car to themselves. This drew more loud protests from the people waiting for their turn to get edited, but not one of them left their spot in line, having learned their lesson from the impulsive teenager.

Tony told everyone to rest their eyes the moment their tram began to move. "There's nothing the edited can do if they take over your body on here," he said. Even though the trip was short, they could catch a quick refresh before they got to the island.

When Shada closed her eyes, she saw Chloe's poisoned body lying on the ground in her mind's eye. She remembered the sound of the gunshot, and the glass breaking, and her breath caught in her throat as she recalled jumping from the moving tram into the water below. She tried counting to ten breaths, hoping the memory would go away, but when it persisted, she opened her eyes to escape into the present.

The pull of eyes burning into the back of her head caused

her to turn around. Some of the unedited in the next car had their faces pressed against the glass separating the two cars and appeared to be trying to kill her with their gaze. Was it possible to cause physical harm if enough people focused their hatred on a single person?

The tram emerged from the underground tunnel that ran beneath the city and rose to the level of the bridge. The city in the background was bathed in the red of the rising sun. Shada turned away from the city, away from the murderous unedited, and watched the island approach.

Shada's car, at the front of the tram, entered the station beneath WestCorp first. The opening doors woke up everyone but Gustavo. The unedited rushed to get out after their eternal wait. Everyone wanted to get their edits first, not knowing they would be led into a massive warehouse with enough tables to accommodate them all. Shada shook Gustavo awake and told her fellow travelers to wait until the other cars had emptied before they disembarked. A few of the unedited stared at them, looking like they might approach, before they rejoined their cohort and headed towards the staircase and its guards.

"Please step off," a robotic voice commanded.

Tony looked at Shada, and she tilted her head towards the platform. They all got off, and she told them to wait until the rest of the unedited had passed through security at the foot of the staircase. "We don't need to get near them," she said.

Everyone wanting edits was past security in minutes. Nobody had to be searched off to the side, and any confiscated items were left behind without a fight.

The group of five was alone on the platform with the two guards, one on each side of the platform.

"What are we going to do?" Sophie said. Shada ignored the question at first, assuming it was meant for Tony, but when

Tony didn't respond, she looked at Sophie and saw the woman's eyes were on her.

"We've got to talk to Alfie. He'll tell us where Sikya is," Shada responded.

Shada wondered why there wasn't more WestCorp security. Didn't Ruby know they were coming?

Tony must have been thinking the same thing. "Where is the welcome committee? I thought we'd have to shoot our way in," he said.

"Maybe they assumed we came to get edited," Ophelia suggested.

"Let's just get past these two, and we can figure out what to do in the food court," Gustavo said. His speech was slow, each word measured, as if he hadn't quite woken up yet.

"But if we don't blow past these guys, they're going to take our guns," Sophie said.

"Let's get as far as we can before we start negotiating," said Tony.

Ophelia laughed at Tony's euphemism.

Sophie pushed back. "If they take our guns, we won't have anything to negotiate with," she said.

Gustavo started walked towards the two large guards. They stood in the distance like two massive pillars supporting the island on their shoulders.

Shada and the others were quick to follow behind, assuming he had a plan. The guards told them to place their bags on a conveyor belt, alongside a bin that was for their belongings, so they could be taken through a metal detector.

Without hesitation, Gustavo threw his bag on the belt and took his guns from their holsters, placing them into the designated bins. Sophie's eyes were wide with disbelief.

"You know we have to keep these," the guard working the

metal detector said, holding up one of Gustavo's guns before starting the conveyor belt.

Gustavo shrugged. Sophie looked like she was going to scream.

The other guard patted down Gustavo and let him pass. The guard working the metal detector looked up from the screen at Gustavo, then at the others. His eyes narrowed. "We'll be keeping the bag," he said, as if tempting someone to offer resistance to his statement. A slight smile crept onto his face, as if he'd relish a fight.

"That's fine," Gustavo said, carefree. He was waved through and began climbing the stairs instead of waiting for the others.

"Gustavo!" Tony said. When his comrade didn't respond, Tony joked that he must be hungry.

Ophelia and Sophie laughed, but Shada grew suspicious.

The rest of the group passed through security in the same way Gustavo had, each forced to leave their bags and weapons behind. Tony made sure Sophie didn't resist. Once everyone was through, they climbed the stairs together.

The food court had been transformed. There was now just one place to eat, a burger spot in the corner, and the rest of the spaces except one were used to process the unedited arrivals from the city. The last space had a large sign above it that read DEPARTURES, with shelves stocked with small vials of Stim to be handed out to those headed back to the city.

Shada, Tony, Sophie, and Ophelia walked around the entire space, inspecting every line of unedited waiting to be processed and enduring their angry stares. Gustavo was nowhere to be found.

"Where the hell did he go?" Tony said. "Let's find Alfie and find out where they're keeping Sikya."

Shada didn't know what they would do if they found her sister. Negotiate her release? It seemed like their lone option, since they were trapped on the island without weapons. Following Gustavo had been a terrible idea.

The departure station was the one place where a WestCorp employee could be approached without navigating past a group of unedited. Shada marched to the counter and asked if they could tell her where to find Alfie.

"Scientists are to stay in the lab until everyone is edited," the employee said, as if they had been forced to recite this rule over and over again until it was committed to memory.

"Even Alfie?" Tony asked.

"He's a scientist, right?" came the reply, with a grin.

Shada shook her head and turned away. She tried to leave the atrium, to take a transport vehicle to the lab, but was stopped by two guards stationed outside. She then tried to lead them down the long hallway, to get to the lab on foot, and found two guards also blocking this path. They were told to wait with the others, that they would all walk to the lab together.

Shada, Tony, Ophelia, and Sophie passed through processing then waited with the other unedited outside the hallway that led to the lab, all of them with paperwork in hand. The unedited stared at them, frozen by the uncertainty of what to do now that Shada and the three members of the resistance were within arm's reach.

Two WestCorp employees emerged from the hallway. They began inspecting everyone's paperwork, nodding when each person could pass. When they were almost to Shada, they stopped and turned to the far side of the atrium, towards the corner that housed the burger restaurant.

Shada turned to see what had stolen their attention.

It was Ruby, her chin held high in the air, with Gustavo at her side.

CHAPTER TWENTY-THREE

RUBY WAS WEARING AN ALL-BLACK outfit accented with bright pink high heels. She strode through the space with the confidence of a woman who was positive she would get what she wanted. Together with Gustavo, dressed in all black himself, she stood out among the run-down unedited from the city and the employees of WestCorp dressed in khakis and white polos.

Gustavo searched the crowd, his head on a swivel.

Shada turned around, nudged Tony, and used her chin to gesture towards Ruby.

"What the hell," Tony whispered.

Ophelia and Sophie, standing behind Shada and Tony, gasped when they saw Ruby and Gustavo. Shada held a finger to her lips, telling them to be quiet. She gestured for the group to follow her, and she left the line.

A WestCorp employee exited an elevator ahead. Shada closed the distance with a few large steps, walked inside, and held the doors open for the others.

She let the elevator doors shut after they were all inside.

"I can't believe Gustavo turned on us!" Sophie exclaimed when they were alone.

"He didn't," Shada said. The button for the second level wouldn't light up when pressed because a key card was required. "They didn't have this before," she said, looking around. "They really don't want anyone leaving the atrium."

The elevator stayed still. It was just a matter of time until they were discovered.

"What do you mean he didn't?" Sophie hissed. "You saw him with Ruby!"

"It wasn't Gustavo," Ophelia said. Her voice was soft, and she seemed preoccupied, as if seeing Gustavo with Ruby had triggered her own memories of losing control.

"It was, I just saw him!" Sophie said.

Shada looked at the buttons above the door, hoping the floor beneath her would soon move and the light corresponding to another level, any level, would blink on, just not the one where they were.

"The edited mind inside him took over," Tony said.

Sophie leaned against the interior of the elevator. "When he fell asleep on the way over," she said.

"I had a feeling when he walked up the steps without us," Shada said.

"Why didn't you say anything?" Tony said. "We could have been more careful."

"If there was going to be a welcome party, Gustavo walking away didn't change anything. Ruby has to know we're here; the trams keep record of everyone who comes to the island."

"Maybe she thinks we really are here to get the edits. Think she just wanted to talk?" Ophelia said.

The sudden descent of the elevator interrupted their conversation. Shada assumed they would end up back on the platform below the atrium, and she pictured their next series of moves. They would climb the stairs once more, somehow get past Ruby, talk to Alfie, and find out where Sikya was being kept. But how would they get her off the island?

It occurred to Shada that Sikya might be in Hollis's private bunker. It was secluded and had the medical equipment she would need.

The elevator's speed, and the length of time it traveled down, seemed far too long to cover the distance between the platform and the atrium. Shada consulted the edited minds inside her, asking if there was anything else beneath them besides the platform.

"It's where—" Marnie said before she was cut off by Hollis.

"Don't tell her, she'll find out soon enough," Hollis said, laughing.

The lit-up button above the elevator door changed with a loud beep, showing U1. The now-lit button was right next to the one corresponding to the ground floor, misaligned with the length of their descent.

A set of doors behind the group, unnoticed by all up to this point, opened up. When Shada turned around, she saw rows upon rows of white pods, each large enough to keep a person inside, in a massive, low-ceilinged room that disappeared into the horizon. Above each pod was a single hanging light bulb. Most of the bulbs closest to them were off, but some were lit, interspersed throughout the grid, and the ones in the distance all shone bright. Fluorescent lights ran down each aisle between rows, creating lines on the ceiling that stretched off into the distance away from the elevator.

A wizened old man stood right in front of them. His thick glasses were too big for his face, and his wool socks were pulled up so high the darker-colored heel could be seen halfway up his calf. He studied the group, blinking twice, before he turned around and shuffled away, leaning on his cane as he went. "I'll just go ahead and stay for another hour," he said with his back turned.

Shada, Tony, Ophelia, and Sophie stepped off the elevator and looked around in awe. There was an empty desk right next to the elevator. Shada watched the old man climb into a white pod a few rows away. The single light above him went out soon after he shut the lid.

Through Marnie, Shada found out they were among rows of dream stations, where the elder edited humans went to pass their days after WestCorp no longer had use for them. Someone was supposed to be at the desk to assign users to unoccupied stations.

"The ones with lights off have someone inside them," Shada told the group after learning the information from Marnie.

"Inside them?" Sophie said. "What are they?"

"Right," Shada said, annoyed at herself for assuming everyone knew what the pods were for. "These are the dream stations, where retired edited go to escape reality."

"Instead of hijacking an unedited body," Ophelia said.

The elevator came back to life behind them. They heard it rise up and pass through the ceiling.

"Do they know we're here?" asked Sophie.

"Not sure, but I don't want to be standing here if they do," Tony replied.

Shada told everyone to hide inside a station. They rushed to the closest illuminated pod. When they found it empty, Tony told Sophie to get inside. Sophie flexed her jaw before climbing in, putting her duffel bag down by her feet.

Shada set the dial beneath the handle to an hour. Along the seam where the lid met the base, they could see a faint purple light begin at Sophie's feet and work its way up to her head, extinguishing when it reached the end of the pod. The single bulb above the pod grew dark the moment the purple light went out.

The process was repeated in another part of the room for Ophelia, before Shada and Tony went to a third available pod. "Climb in," Tony told Shada.

"No, I'll be the last one," she said.

They stared each other down.

"How are you going to turn off the light above?" Tony asked.

Shada licked her fingers and unscrewed the bulb just enough for the electrical connection to sever. "Like that," she said.

"Perfect," Tony said. "You lie in here, and I'll do the same thing before I climb into one of those over there," he said, gesturing to the side of the room farthest from the elevator.

Shada smiled. "Get in, Tony," she said.

Tony's head cocked to one side, searching Shada's face. She waited, focusing on her breath to slow her heart rate. Tony squeezed his lips together and climbed in, his duffel bag positioned between his legs.

"Leave it off, I want to hear when they come for us," Tony said.

Shada, her hand on the pod's lid, nodded. "You got it," she said before closing the lid. She walked around Tony's pod and set her bag on the floor without a noise. Then she climbed over the white pod, draping her body over it, and reached down for the timer from above.

"Shada?" Tony said from inside.

She felt him push against the lid and went limp so all her weight would be used to keep it shut. She set the timer for four hours.

When the purple light began at Tony's feet, Shada heard him scream her name. He pushed against the lid, struggling to get free, until the light extinguished at his head and his movement stopped.

"Sorry," she said before climbing down.

Shada hurried back to Sophie's and Ophelia's pods and changed the setting of the timers from one hour to four. She apologized both times.

She was close enough to the elevator to hear its descent. She turned and ran away as fast as she could, sticking to one side of the room, an aisle out of direct sight of the elevator. Over the sound of her breathing, she heard the beep that accompanied the opening of the elevator's doors, so she crouched down while continuing forward. There had to be another way out, and she intended to find it.

She heard Ruby yell out, "Find them!"

She kept running, amazed at the length of the room. She felt like she ran the length of the entirety of the island and wondered if she was deep enough underground to run beneath the water around the island. A timer beneath one of the lone dead light bulbs ahead of Shada went off, and when the buzzing stopped, the light above came back to life.

Shada saw a thin, age-spotted hand lift the lid of the pod, the interior hidden by the surrounding machines. She ran past, hoping the person didn't see her. She waited to hear if the dreamer yelled out, but all she heard was her breathing.

At the end of the room were double doors with small windows set at head height in the middle of each. She pushed through and found an old metal staircase. It had cracked, decayed brown tile and green metal latticework beneath each railing. There was a door opposite where she'd entered at the bottom of the stairs. She looked inside and found the remains of a collapsed building. It was tight, but she could have navigated through the rubble if she didn't have her bag with her. To throw her pursuers off her scent, she left her bag just inside the rubble, hoping it would seem like she'd left it behind before crawling through.

Shada ran up the stairs, covering two at a time. She lost track of how many times she turned the corner and started a new section. She felt how little she had slept and eaten in the past two days. From her playing days, she knew there were extra reserves the body could call on at the end of the game, when it was all on the line, but she also knew these wouldn't last forever. She counted her breaths in order to escape from the monotony of the climb and to make sure the edited minds inside her, in particular Hollis, didn't take advantage of her exhausted state to try to retake control of her body.

She passed by a source of daylight at the bottom of a window well and slowed down, knowing she had returned to the surface. The staircase ended at the top of the next set of stairs. There was a single door, with a single window at head height. She looked through one corner of the window and saw a woman rushing down the hall, her head down and white lab coat fluttering at her feet.

CHAPTER TWENTY-FOUR

SHADA PUSHED OPEN the door at the top of the stairs and walked into the lab's hallway. The section of the lab she was in was older than the parts she had been to before. The floors were a dull off-white with brown specks, and the walls were a mustard yellow with thin cobwebs up near the ceiling. She hoped her lack of white coat wouldn't draw attention from any of the WestCorp employees. She stood tall, doing her best to seem like she belonged there.

Her first thought was to figure out where she was. She knew she was in the lab, but which part? She didn't recognize any of the rooms around her. She peeked into the closest room. It was empty, with a variety of glassware scattered on the counters. The shelves above each counter held bottles of all different shapes and sizes, all labeled with a uniform sticker and the writing in the same color ink.

"This is the chemistry wing," Hollis said before Shada could search his memories. "Where they worked on the Stim, at least when I was still in charge."

When Shada withdrew from the room, she found a man in a

lab coat walking down the hallway in her direction. She got ready to pretend she was lost.

"Can I help you?" the scientist said. He smiled when he spoke. It seemed he enjoyed talking to another human, even though she was a potential trespasser.

"I'm looking for the room to get edited." She pulled her paperwork from her pocket, hoping to convince him she had gotten lost, that she was at the lab to receive her free edits. This seemed easier than convincing him she was edited as well.

"It isn't hard," Marnie told Shada. "Just smile. Nobody can tell the difference."

The scientist didn't even glance down at the paper in Shada's hand. "You're a long way from the rest of the unedited," he said.

Shada couldn't tell if the man was suspicious or not. That smile did more to mask his thoughts than if he'd tried to remain impartial.

"Can you tell me how to get back to them?" Shada asked, doing her best to sound innocent. She reasoned that Alfie would be with the unedited, overseeing their edits.

"Sure. You must have been walking for a while; we aren't even close."

"I'm very lost," she said with a laugh.

The scientist told her to walk in the direction from which he'd come. There, she would find another hallway running perpendicular to the one they were in. "Turn left, then keep walking until it ends too. A right turn will take you to where the edits are taking place."

Shada thanked the man and set off. She turned around every few steps, to see if the scientist was watching her walk away, but he continued at his steady pace until he turned off the hallway, either down another or into a room.

There was a definite change in the quality of the building

when she left the chemistry wing. The walls became newer, stark white, and matched the white floors, which had been buffed to a shine. The air smelled of sterility, a mix of bleach and lemon soap. As she continued on the scientist's suggested path, there were more and more scientists rushing between rooms, each of them carrying manila folders stuffed with papers.

The low rumble from a large crowd of people reached her when she got to the end of the hallway and turned right.

Shada recognized where she was. The first time she'd come to get edited, before the edits were free, she was led to the large warehouse room, ahead of her on the left, where the unedited were now gathered. This was before she and Chloe had been asked if they would accept an uploaded mind into their body so WestCorp employees could experience the world in an unedited body. She also knew where Alfie's personal lab was. She made her way there, hoping to find him and find out where her sister was being kept.

The door to Alfie's lab was unlocked. Shada walked in without knocking. He wasn't inside, but she could tell this was where a lot of his time was spent; on the counter was trash from prior meals next to scattered paperwork and evidence of chemical experiments he hadn't bothered to clean up.

She guessed he was with the unedited, either preparing them for or performing their edits. Even if she left the lab and found him, what was she supposed to do? Tap him on the shoulder and ask for a private word? No, she needed him to come to her. Her sister had already been gone long enough, and she didn't have time to wait.

The bottles of chemicals drew her attention. Shada inspected each one, not sure of what she was looking for. A gallon jug of benzene caught her eye. It had a large "flammable" symbol on it.

There was a momentary pause when Shada was hit by the

potential consequences of what she was about to do. But her sister was worth it.

Shada assembled all the chemicals in a pile on the side of the room farthest from the door. She opened the jug of benzene and poured it out over the containers. Her eyes watered from the fumes. She kept them closed until the jug was empty, then backed away, looking for a way to spark the blaze. She was searching for matches or a lighter when she found an old Bunsen burner and a long piece of rubber tubing. After locating the gas line and connecting the rubber to one end, she set the burner, unlit, on the ground. She still had the same problem as before: How to spark the blaze?

The smell of benzene began to overwhelm her as it suffused throughout the room. She looked in the cabinet where she'd found the Bunsen burner and found a striker, a piece of flint and steel at one end of a pair of tongs that when squeezed created a spark. She tested it out and saw a small spark. A momentary fear gripped her, soon followed by relief, when she realized she had created a spark in the midst of the fumes.

She turned on the gas and fell to her hands and knees, lighting the Bunsen burner before more fumes crept from the pile of chemicals. By using the rubber tubing to force the burner along the ground, she was able to get it close to the benzene. Nothing happened.

Impatient, she twisted the rubber tube, knocking over the burner. The benzene ignited in a bright flash, causing small colored lights to appear in Shada's vision.

She hurried to turn off the gas so the flame wouldn't travel through the rubber tube to the gas source. Once the gas was off, she turned over the stainless steel table closest to the door and waited for the containers holding the other chemicals to melt, hoping some of their contents would explode.

The fire alarm and sprinkler system kicked into action. A

torrent of water rushed down from the ceiling, and Shada worried the fire would be extinguished before it could catch anything else on fire. She watched one container melt without its contents bursting into flames and was about to stand up when a plastic bottle erupted in a fireball. She pulled her head back behind the table just in time.

The door burst open, and Alfie rushed into the room. He was drenched. The howling fire alarm overhead was deafening. Shada rushed the older scientist and pinned him against the wall, her hands around his throat.

"Where's Sikya?" she screamed. Water was dripping down her face.

"My work! Let me put out the fire!" Alfie responded. He tried to push himself off the wall, but Shada was stronger than him and forced him back down. "The fire extinguisher!" he yelled.

"Where is she?" Shada said. She was losing control and she knew it. She forced herself to exhale so she could keep Hollis and Marnie from taking over her body.

Alfie squirmed. "In Hollis's bunker. She's safe, the baby's safe. Now let me go!"

This time, when Alfie tried to pry himself free, Shada didn't stop him. She watched him rush to the far wall, grab the fire extinguisher, and position himself right in front of the fire.

A glass bottle exploded right before he squeezed the trigger. Flames and glass went everywhere. Shada got a few cuts on her arms and legs but knew none of them were serious. Alfie, standing between her and the explosion, had taken the majority of the blast. He was on the floor, his torso burning. Shada grabbed the fire extinguisher and put out the flames on Alfie, then the chemicals, covering them all with a thick white foam. She dropped to his side. There were deep cuts all over his face and neck. Blood was pouring out from him, creating deep red lines in the foam, surrounded by bright pink.

"I would have told you where she was," he sputtered. Blood trickled from the corner of his mouth.

"I know," Shada said. Her guilt was almost unmanageable. She'd never meant to hurt Alfie, the one person who had helped her take back control. His motivation was science, not because he cared for her, but she didn't care about the reason. The fact was that he'd helped her and was now dying because of her.

It was Chloe all over again. Was she destined to be responsible for the deaths of those closest to her?

"I still have more to do," Alfie said. The sprinkler system, sensing the fire was no longer blazing, shut off.

"I know," Shada said again. She couldn't tell if the salty taste in her mouth was her own tears or water that had run down her unwashed face.

"Let me upload into you. We can rescue your sister together, then we can figure out how to continue my work," Alfie said. He was growing weaker by the second and didn't have much time.

Hollis tried voicing his objections, but Shada silenced him in less than a heartbeat. She had already been responsible for Chloe's death and wasn't going to lose Alfie too.

CHAPTER TWENTY-FIVE

"WE'LL NEVER MAKE it to the upload room," Shada told Alfie. Even if the lab was empty and she didn't have to navigate past other scientists, there was no way she could carry him that far. He was losing a lot of blood and could pass out at any second.

"Here," Alfie choked out. "Prototype."

Between the overturned stainless steel table and another table was a small monitor with an attached keyboard. Its back was covered by clear plastic, protecting the visible wires from getting wet. The fire and fire extinguisher foam had been far enough away that the machine was left untouched. Two long cables, covered in rubber, were attached, one on each side. The ends of the cables didn't end in helmets; they each ended with two electrodes, which was why Shada hadn't known there was a mind transfer machine in the room before Alfie told her.

Shada put her arms under the scientist, one under his shoulders and the other under his knees. Some of the foam stained with blood transferred onto her. She counted down from three, both to make sure Alfie was ready for the pain and to prepare herself for the exertion. After the count of one, she took a deep breath and pushed into the floor with her feet, standing up with him in her arms.

When she was halfway to standing, Hollis tried to take back over. Shada felt him open her hands. She was straining so hard she couldn't take back control. She used her arms to keep the dying scientist in place but couldn't rise any further.

Through squinted eyes, she saw her hands close. It wasn't her own doing, since her connection with the appendages was still blocked by Hollis.

"Leave her alone!" Marnie said.

Shada stood up with Marnie's help. She took small steps to the middle of the three tables and laid him down. She placed her hands on her knees, taking deep breaths. "Asshole," she said out loud, sure Hollis could hear. "Thanks, Marnie."

Alfie's head rolled to one side. His chest rose and fell with short breaths, but his body was otherwise limp.

Shada rounded the table Alfie was on and flipped up the table she had used for cover before. She attached the electrodes to Alfie's head, one on each temple, before attaching them in the same position on herself. She turned on the monitor between the tables and saw lines of white computer script begin filling the black screen from the top down. The oldest script disappeared at the bottom as more appeared at the top, seeming to go on forever. Eventually, a prompt appeared at the top of the screen: type T for transfer and S for storage.

Shada typed T, then selected L to tell the system the mind to be uploaded was coming from the left. A countdown from ten appeared on the screen, the lower number appearing above the higher one in a vertical line.

"Hold on," Shada told Alfie as she lay down. She felt Hollis attempt to take back control of her arm one last time, but she forced him into the background before he ever gained control of the limb.

Her world went black.

She allowed the light to take over her awareness. She soon recognized the ceiling above her bed, and the second the edges of darkness disappeared, she heard the blaring fire alarm. Then she was aware of her body once again. The scientist's mind was pushed back into the abyss. She heard him screaming in the darkness and told him to be quiet.

Marnie and Hollis were locked in a struggle for control that ended as soon as Shada was back. It was easy for her to block the two minds, like two small children trying to fight an adult and once the adult decided it was over, there was nothing the children could do.

"He tried to run the second you disappeared," Marnie said.

"Why are you helping her?" Hollis roared.

"We're stuck in here. Why fight it?" Marnie said. "We might as well work together."

"Work together to destroy everything I built? Never!"

Shada silenced both of them. She stared at the ceiling and focused on helping Alfie.

"Find the light and go to it," she said. "And you'll be able to see the world through my eyes."

Shada could sense Alfie understood.

"Do you see it?" Shada said a moment later.

"No," Alfie said.

Shada knew he was scared. "Give it time," she said.

"It's faint. Every time I find it, I lose it right away."

"Look around it, like looking at a faint star. It will grow brighter."

Shada waited until Alfie told her the light was staying in his awareness. When he reported it was growing bigger, she asked about the prompt for storage on the monitor.

"Was that in preparation for when the computer engineer

solved the problem?" Shada asked, not wanting to get her hopes up that the solution had been found.

"He already solved it. We can store minds on this device. It's the only one."

Shada felt a wave of excitement wash over her. Her first thought was to help Tony and give Sikya the family her sister deserved.

"Why didn't you have me store your mind on the device instead?" Shada asked.

"I can't continue my work from inside a machine," Alfie responded. "There's still a lot I want to do." He told her the circle of light was getting larger. "What happens next?"

"Once the ring of darkness disappears, you'll be able to hear the world too. Over time, there will be an awareness of my limbs as well, but don't bother trying to take over. If I don't block you, Marnie will."

"I won't bother. I'll have to guide you through my experiments." He then informed Shada he could hear the fire alarm.

"Welcome back," Shada said.

"You mentioned Marnie. Can I communicate with her? With Hollis?"

"Do it in the background. I don't need or want the distraction."

"Fair enough," Alfie said. "Can I see my old body?"

Shada turned her head to the side. Even this small action took an enormous amount of effort, and she became aware of how exhausted her body was. Thoughts of Sikya flashed through her head, and she knew she had to continue on and get her off the island.

Alfie's chest still rose and fell with each short sip of air. As they watched, his breathing became rapid then stopped altogether.

"I'm sorry," Shada told Alfie.

Alfie didn't say a word.

Shada heard a loud click and knew it came from the real world, that the noise wasn't in her head. She turned, sat up, and stared straight down the barrel of a gun. Gustavo's finger was on the trigger.

Ruby emerged from behind him, disdain on her face as she inspected the destruction of the lab.

"What did you think this would accomplish?" Ruby said.

Shada responded with silence. She watched as the leader of WestCorp knelt over Alfie, checking to see if he was still breathing.

Ruby shook her head when she realized the scientist was dead. "I thought you would come to get your sister. I never imagined you'd end up in here. What were you trying to do?"

Gustavo answered Ruby's question in a deadpan voice. "She came to stop us from editing the people from the city," he said. It wasn't Gustavo; it was whoever was uploaded into his body, having taken over during his nap on the tram.

Ruby laughed. "This didn't even make a dent! The edits will still continue, once we clean up all the water." She plucked the electrodes off Alfie's skull. Her face fell, and she looked at Shada. "He's in your head now, isn't he?" she said.

Shada didn't see the point in denying the truth. She nodded.

"Interesting way to try to stop me," Ruby said. "Were you trying to prevent us from developing better technology? It won't save the others from the city, but it could help those in the future . . ." Her voice trailed off. "The kid!" she said in a flash of recognition. "You want to make sure the future isn't any worse for your sister's baby." Ruby shook her head. "I admire your long-term thinking, but it still won't help." Ruby then told Gustavo to push Alfie's body off the table, holding her hands up and contorting her face, signaling she didn't want to get dirty.

Gustavo walked over and used his left hand to push the

scientist off the table while his right hand still held the gun pointed at Shada. Alfie's body fell to the floor with the loud crunch of broken bones, settling in a jumbled heap.

Ruby sat on the edge of the table that was covered in blood. "I can't let you keep Alfie," she said. "He belongs to WestCorp, and therefore belongs to me. You're going to upload him into my body," Ruby said. She looked at Shada, delighted, waiting to see what resistance awaited her.

Shada sighed. "What about Hollis? You don't have a problem letting me keep him."

Ruby looked like she'd been slapped. "I . . . I . . . I don't want him inside my head," she stammered.

"I think you like being in charge of WestCorp," Shada shot back. "What if I told you he doesn't have to be in your head, that he can stay on the island?"

Ruby's eyes narrowed. "Elaborate."

"This is a prototype for mind transfer," Shada said. "And storage."

Inside Shada's head, Alfie scolded Shada for giving away knowledge of the device. She silenced him.

"So you could upload Michael onto this machine," Ruby said, looking at the monitor. "And Alfie as well?"

"Sure, they can both be on there."

Ruby told Shada to put Hollis into storage. This time, when prompted by the monitor, Shada chose S and was shown another prompt: type L for left and R for right, accompanied by arrows.

Shada laughed, wondering who would be playing around with uploaded consciousnesses without being able to discern left from right.

She typed R, and a countdown began. She wondered how the machine would be able to determine which of the three minds inside her got uploaded. One appeared on the screen, and she pushed Alfie and Marnie into the darkness before joining them, leaving Hollis in control of her body for the final second.

When she returned to the light, she knew Hollis was gone. "There," she said to Ruby.

"Do the same thing with Alfie," Gustavo commanded.

"Let's not get ahead of ourselves," Ruby said. "Alfie doesn't do me any good inside a machine. I need him to continue his work." She inspected Gustavo. "And if we upload him into you, there's a chance your host will take back over."

"I wouldn't let that happen."

"Maybe not, but it's still a chance." Ruby paused for a moment. "The only option is to upload him into me. I'll continue his work myself."

The leader of WestCorp placed the two electrodes onto her temples and lay down in Alfie's blood.

CHAPTER TWENTY-SIX

ALFIE ACCEPTED that his mind would be transferred into Ruby, and Shada felt him try to take over her body during the countdown. The rest of the room was silent. Ruby's eyes were closed while she waited to accept Alfie's mind, and Gustavo held his gun pointed at Shada.

Alfie began to panic. "I can't find any part of your body," he said, communicating to Shada through thoughts.

"That's because I'm not letting you," Shada responded.

"Don't I have to be in control to transfer?"

Shada told Alfie he was correct, the way a teacher might tell a struggling student he was on the right path. She sensed the countdown was almost finished.

"You can't!" Marnie screamed when she realized what Shada was about to do.

"Try to work together," Shada told the pair of edited minds. Marnie tried to sacrifice herself by taking control of Shada's body, but Shada blocked her too.

She had made the decision to upload herself into Ruby, and there was nothing either of the uploaded minds could do about it. Her world went black.

Waking up in another's body was a new sensation. She expected to see the light in the distance, to wait for it to take over her field of vision, but instead she woke up with Ruby in the background. She remembered how Hollis had been in charge of her body after his upload, before she found the light and took back control. Now she would have to deal with Ruby's attempts to do the same.

Shada sat up. Seeing her previous body on the table next to her gave her the sense of being in a surreal dream. She noticed the thin red scars running down her cheeks from when Hollis had cut her face with a razor, attempting to make her cry tears of blood. It seemed like so long ago that she was in the bathroom without control of herself, and she promised herself she would look in the mirror more often so she would never forget.

"Ruby?" Gustavo asked. Whoever was in charge of the man's body should have known how long it took for the host to take back control from an uploaded mind. Either they forgot, or they had unfounded faith in Ruby's capabilities.

Shada, inside Ruby's body, ignored the question. She tossed her legs over the edge of the table, closed her eyes, and took a series of long, slow breaths.

She heard Gustavo tell Shada to stay down. Then, more people arrived in the lab. Ruby's eyes stayed closed, but Shada heard Gustavo tell them to wait. The additional people fanned out in the room, and Shada knew they all belonged to the island.

She was her own moment of calm in the eye of the storm.

Ruby discovered the circle of light and lost it every time she tried to focus on it. She went through the cycle of losing it and finding it countless times, iterations of a process independent of time. Frustrated, she screamed out Alfie's name.

Shada-in-Ruby smiled.

"She's back!" Gustavo said, mistaking the smile for his leader's return from the darkness.

The fire alarm stopped blaring, and Shada opened Ruby's eyes. She was surrounded by WestCorp employees, all dressed in khaki pants and a white polo.

Shada-in-Ruby looked at the body next to her once more. The head was turned in her direction, and they locked eyes. Whoever was in charge—either Marnie or Alfie—hadn't told Gustavo that Shada was the one who'd transferred. Shada felt a strange satisfaction knowing the two edited minds were on her side.

"Alfie! Let me come back!" Ruby screamed.

Shada was delighted Ruby still thought the scientist was the one in charge of her body.

Gustavo got the attention of the two WestCorp employees who were closest to Shada's body. He used his eyes to point at the body still lying on the table then tilted his head in the direction of the door, indicating it was time to get her out of here.

"Leave her," Shada-in-Ruby said. "I'm not done with her yet."

Ruby tried a different approach. "Alfie, let me back in so we can continue your work," she said in a sweet, delicate way. Shada could sense the rage present behind the words and wondered if Ruby realized that none of her thoughts or feelings would ever be secret again.

Shada closed her eyes, leaving the fire-ravaged room and its occupants behind. "Ruby," she thought. "I can hear you."

Shada got immense pleasure from Ruby's disbelief.

"You . . ." Ruby said. The woman's rage before was nothing compared to its magnitude when she heard Shada's voice from inside her own body.

"It's me."

"You're blocking me from taking back over my own body!" Ruby said.

"I don't have to; you don't even know how to get it back."

"You're scared if I regain control, you won't be able to take back over."

Shada thought the woman's amateur attempt at reverse psychology was cute. She opened Ruby's eyes and looked at Ruby's spotted, wrinkled hand, devoid of adornment.

"Allow the light to take over your vision."

"What do you think I've been trying to do?" Ruby snarled.

"You've been trying to force it. You have to allow it."

"What's the difference?" Ruby's mind grew still. "Why are you helping me?" she asked.

"I want you to see what I'm about to do." She waited for the light to take over Ruby's awareness.

When Ruby again saw the world through her own eyes, and heard the world through her own ears, she tried to scream out to the forces in the room whose feet could be seen through her peripheral vision. Shada never allowed Ruby to reconnect to her body, so these thoughts fizzled out before reaching her tongue.

"Do you see your hand?" Shada asked Ruby.

"Yes."

Shada withdrew her connection to the limb, allowing Ruby to take it over.

"Do you feel your hand?"

Shada watched as the fingers on the hand began to move. The thumb tapped the tops of each finger then made a fist. As Shada watched, the middle finger rose up, and the palm turned to face her.

Shada laughed before taking back control and relaxing the hand. She heard Gustavo laugh too, followed by the rest of the people in the room.

"Alfie's trying to take back over, huh?" Gustavo said.

"Idiot," Ruby said. Nobody but Shada could hear her.

Shada felt Ruby try to take back control of the hand. She let Ruby get close before forcing her back into the darkness.

"I can keep you there as long as I want," Shada thought.

"This isn't even hard for you, is it?" Ruby said, both frustrated and in awe.

"Not even a little."

"Are the others this good?" Ruby asked.

Shada probed Ruby's thoughts, searching to see if her deference was hiding a more sinister motivation. There was plenty of hate in the older woman's thoughts, but none of it scheming. "I've got the best handle on things," Shada said.

Ruby wondered if it was something to do with the fact Shada was unedited. She didn't have to communicate the thought to Shada, because Shada was aware of all that went through the woman's mind.

"Only one unedited ever had a problem with an edited mind," Shada said. "Richard. And I'm positive that if I was the one to teach him how to take back control, he'd still be alive."

"Let's find out what makes the unedited so good at controlling their bodies!" Ruby said. "Stay on the island, and we can study how to make you even better."

"It's not that we're good at controlling our bodies. We're good at controlling our emotions. Because we have them, we're born with them, and we learn to manage them our entire lives. WestCorp can't make this better; the skill is too delicate. All their fingerprints can do is destroy."

Shada knew it was time to get rid of Ruby for good. She looked up at Gustavo with Ruby's eyes. "Taking back control from one mind wasn't so hard."

Gustavo's eyes grew wide, as if he'd been slapped across the face. "I'm sorry it took so long for me to figure it out," he stammered.

Shada-in-Ruby laughed. "That wasn't an attack. What I'm saying is I don't see why I can't try to hold another! If she"—

Shada-in-Ruby looked at Shada's body on the table with all the scorn she could muster—"can control two, then so can I!"

Whoever had taken control of Shada's previous body, either Marnie or Alfie, inspected Ruby's face. Their eyes grew wide with worry as they stared, a frantic search to see if it was Ruby or Shada in control of the leader's body.

Shada-in-Ruby told her former self there was nothing to worry about. "We'll transfer Marnie, and you'll be left alone in there, free from the extra minds. Your body will be yours again," she said, pretending her own mind was still in her own body and not inside Ruby. She hoped none of the WestCorp employees would realize what she was about to do. A moment later she added, "After that, I'll take you to your sister. It'll be just the two of you!"

The other members of WestCorp all laughed.

Shada-in-Ruby lay down on the table and twisted so she could reach the monitor. She selected S, for storage, then L, to designate the mind was coming from her side of the monitor. The countdown began, and she rested her head on the table with her eyes closed.

"Wait!" Gustavo said. "It says S on the screen . . . that's the option she chose when she put Hollis into storage!"

Shada turned Ruby's head and opened her eyes. Gustavo allowed his weapon's aim to fall as he rushed towards the monitor.

Marnie or Alfie—whoever controlled Shada—shot up and lunged for the man. They fought as the seconds passed. Gustavo ended up on top, holding her down with his knee and both hands on the gun now aimed at her chest. He couldn't make it to the monitor in time to stop the countdown.

"Take those off!" he yelled to Shada-in-Ruby. His eyes fluttered between the two electrodes on her head.

Shada looked at the monitor and saw two appear on the screen. She closed her eyes and plunged into the darkness, forcing Ruby into the light.

CHAPTER TWENTY-SEVEN

THE AWARENESS of the room returned to Shada, her mind now the sole resident in Ruby's body. Gustavo stared at her.

"What happened?" he said, his eyes narrowed with suspicion.

Shada couldn't lie and say Marnie had transferred into her. She looked at the ceiling with Ruby's eyes, pretending to scan her internal state for signs of other consciousnesses. "I'm alone in here," she said.

"The monitor was set for storage," Gustavo said. "That's why I told you to take off those wires." He used his chin to gesture to both her temples.

Shada-in-Ruby nodded.

"But who got uploaded?" he asked. He put his left hand on the ground, using it to stand up, while his right kept the gun pointed at Shada's former body on the ground. Shada knew the weapon could be aiming at her in the blink of an eye.

"Alfie," Shada-in-Ruby said without hesitation. She got off the table and stood over her previous body. Both electrodes had been torn off in the struggle. "It's a good thing too, she wasn't even attached!"

Gustavo stood a step away, watching who he thought was Ruby help who he thought was Shada stand up.

Alfie or Marnie stared into Shada-in-Ruby's eyes, searching for some sign of recognition. Ruby's left eye displayed the slightest wink. "Let's try this again," Shada-in-Ruby said, loud enough for all around to hear. She helped her former body onto the table once more. "Ready to come live in my body?" she asked.

Either Marnie or Alfie shook Shada's head no.

"Of course not," Gustavo said. It sounded like he was rolling his eyes at the same time.

Shada ignored him. "You'd rather be stuck in there?" Shada-in-Ruby said.

"That one's old. Her time will come soon enough," Shada's former body said. The intonation of the voice was flat, similar to how Alfie spoke. "I want as much time as possible to finish what I started."

Gustavo laughed. "What can you do? Once you're off this table, you'll be thrown in with your sister, away from the rest of the world." He still assumed Shada was the one speaking from inside her own body and seemed to forget his suspicion about who was inside Ruby.

Shada-in-Ruby reattached the electrodes, whispering while their faces were close. "I'm coming back in. Alfie, you don't want to take over Ruby, alone?"

Alfie-in-Shada's head made the slightest shift from left to right.

Shada-in-Ruby stood up straight and turned around, addressing the group of WestCorp employees in the lab with her. "The girl makes a good point," she said. "I'm already old and don't have much time left."

Gustavo's head tilted to one side while he waited for her to continue.

"I think I'll take over her body," Shada-in-Ruby said.

"Your husband already tried that, and look where it got him. He's stuck inside a machine!" Gustavo replied.

Shada-in-Ruby looked at him and smirked. "Sounds like you don't think I can do it."

"It's not worth it."

"But I have one thing Michael didn't: the ability to upload. I'll get in there, then we can upload her mind into storage, leaving me alone!"

Gustavo looked around, aware that he was pushing back against the leader of the company in front of other employees. "She won't be the one who ends up in storage."

"What are you saying?"

"Shada's too good. If you go in there and try to put her into storage, she'll find a way to make sure you're the one going into the machine." He paused, took a deep breath, and seemed to come up with a solution. "Why don't we upload her mind now? Then you can take over her body."

Shada-in-Ruby didn't want to admit it, but his suggestion made sense. She set aside her reservations, agreed, then turned back to her former body. Gustavo expected both Marnie and Shada to be inside. "Don't make me run this more than once. I'll leave your body empty if I have to."

Shada watched as the eyes of her former body blinked twice. The face softened, and she felt deep inside that Marnie was now in control.

Marnie-in-Shada closed her eyes and dropped her chin twice, indicating she was ready to sacrifice herself.

Shada wished she could tell Marnie she would get her out as soon as she could, but there was no way to communicate without everyone else in the room hearing her. She initiated the upload. Seconds later, Alfie-in-Shada opened his eyes and let out a prolonged exhale.

"Finally rid of that filthy unedited!" Alfie-in-Shada said.

The scientist was playing along. Shada felt relief wash over her. Although she doubted Marnie would use such strong language, she also knew the sentiment was common among the edited. She hoped it was enough to convince Gustavo that Shada was in fact gone, leaving Marnie behind, alone.

Alfie-in-Shada's reaction seemed to be enough proof for Gustavo that Shada was gone. "Let's get you transferred over!" he said.

Shada-in-Ruby made sure the electrodes were attached to her own head then set up the monitor to transfer from left to right. She lay down on the table as the countdown began.

Shada didn't want to kill Ruby, but the upload would leave the older woman's body an empty vessel, devoid of life. Without a mind, and with no hope of regaining one, there would be no point for the body to exist. She knew they could keep it alive, for a time, with the technology on the island. How long would it take for the body to expire without any support? Days, from dehydration? Would it be a mercy to kill her sooner?

She thought about Chloe, and Alfie, and how their deaths had come about because of her actions. Both of those deaths had produced a sense of remorse; she felt nothing for Ruby. Not vindication, not relief, just nothing.

Shada's vision went black. When she found the light and opened her eyes, she was back inside her own body.

"Welcome back," Alfie said. "Remember, you're supposed to be Ruby."

Shada, back in her own body, opened her eyes. With just one mind inside her, Alfie, she felt like she could think faster than before.

"Gentlemen," she said, doing her best to sound both commanding and condescending at the same time. It was her best impression of Ruby. "Did everyone hear when our friend here questioned my decision?"

Shada sat up. Alfie laughed, knowing where the conversation was headed.

There were a few nods from the members of the group. "Well? Did you?"

Every WestCorp employee other than Gustavo said they'd heard him.

"Would you do me a favor and remove him from my sight?"

Gustavo, controlled by an edited mind, lowered his weapon to the ground with his other hand in the air, signaling he wasn't going to resist. Two men grabbed him, each one holding an arm.

"Where should we take him?" one of Gustavo's captors said.

"Take him to the bunker. Put two guards outside his door. The biggest ones we have." The two men led a shocked Gustavo away from the lab.

Shada liked giving orders and found herself enjoying the new role. She stood up and pulled the electrodes off of Ruby's mindless body. The woman looked frail as her chest rose and fell. The wrinkles in her face, kept hidden by makeup, made faint lines in her skin even when her face was relaxed.

The remaining WestCorp force, less than a dozen in total, stared at the two women. Ruby's lifeless body still commanded their attention, even though Shada was now in charge.

"Listen," Shada snapped. She jammed her index finger into her chest. "I'm in here now. Get used to it." She asked Alfie, through her thoughts, if it was OK to move the prototype; he said yes. "I need two of you to carry this," she said. She unplugged the monitor from the wall, lifted it up, and placed it on the table she had laid on during the uploads. She wrapped the long electrode wires around her hand and put them on top of the monitor. "The ones who aren't carrying it, guard it with your life."

The men scrambled to follow her orders.

"Wait for me in the hallway. And remember that my husband's in there!" she barked at the men as they left the lab.

Alfie agreed this was a nice touch. "What are you going to do with her?" he asked, referring to Ruby's former body.

"Not a thing," Shada said. She walked out of the lab, looking back once more before she locked the door from the inside and shut it.

She thought of Chloe. If she could leave her friend behind to die, she could do it to Ruby too.

CHAPTER TWENTY-EIGHT

THE MEN in the hallway stared at Shada for direction.

"We're going to the bunker," she said. She led the way through the lab building towards the exit, walking through the standing water left by the sprinkler system.

Outside the building was chaos. Scores of people milled about, waiting to find out what they should do. WestCorp employees had rounded up the inhabitants of the city and made them stand together, gathered around a single palm tree. Everyone was drenched.

Shada wondered if the edits had been completed or if the fire had interrupted the process before it began. She would deal with them later. Her first priority was Sikya.

It took three vehicles to transport Shada and her followers to the bunker at the edge of the island. The chain-link fence still surrounded the entrance, and the towering guards were posted outside. The dog inside the square lifted its head and stared at Shada's group as they approached.

"Hold it right there," one of the guards said while holding a hand up. He was one of two at the entrance, and there were two more posted on each corner.

Shada told them to let her group through.

The two guards at the entrance erupted in laughter. "Why should we listen to you? You were in here yourself not too long ago!"

They looked past Shada and her group, shaking their heads to themselves as if repeating the joke in their minds.

"Let us through," one of the WestCorp employees said. He lowered his voice to a hoarse whisper. "You don't know what you're doing."

"I'm doing my job!" the talkative guard said, looking at the employee with disgust.

"This is Ruby," another WestCorp employee chimed in. "She transferred her mind into this girl's body."

This revelation seemed to get their attention.

"Why do you think we're walking with her?" a third employee said. "We watched it happen. Just now, in the lab. Get out of the way or you'll end up at the bottom of the bay."

Shada wondered if people were ever actually thrown into the water surrounding the island or if it was an idle threat tossed around by the edited. Either way, their attitudes changed.

"Where's Alfie?" the guard said. "Get him here, and he'll tell us the truth." They were used to the scientist going in and out of the bunker, so he was someone they could trust.

"It's too complicated to explain. Just let us in!" a WestCorp employee said.

The guards didn't have the chance to wrap their heads around the situation before Shada walked between them. "I'm going in," she said.

The guards didn't stop her. They took a step back and allowed the other members of her group through.

The brown dog with flecks of gray in his face sauntered up to Shada's side. She reached down and petted his head while she walked. "Hello, Jax," she said. He ran away when they were halfway to the front door, trying to play, but when Shada didn't pay attention to him, he came back to her side and walked with her until they reached the concrete in front of the door. He must have been trained to stay away from the entrance, because he stood outside while Shada and her group went inside.

The elevator couldn't arrive fast enough. It seemed to crawl from the level below until it stopped at their level. The doors crept open as if they were peeling apart to reveal a secret that could escape if startled. Shada walked inside first, followed by the rest. The two men holding the prototype boarded last, facing the door.

Shada pushed her way past the men as soon as the elevator doors opened. She jogged down the bunker's empty corridor, stopping to search in every room. She paused at the padded room where she'd been held captive by Ruby. The door was open just a crack, and the light was on. Keeping a pregnant Sikya confined in the same room in which her sister had been kept seemed like something Ruby would enjoy.

Shada pushed the door open. The heavy door creaked and stopped halfway. The room was empty. She inspected the rest of the rooms and found nothing.

The two WestCorp employees in charge of bringing Gustavo to the bunker were seated across from each other at the long table in the open space at the end of the corridor. The expansive jet-black wall across the back glittered in the artificial light.

"Are you two the only ones here?" Shada asked, worried Sikya wasn't there.

"The guy you told us to bring down is in that room over there," one of the men said, pointing to the upload room to the right of Hollis's bedroom.

"There's a woman in the other room," the second WestCorp employee added.

Shada rushed into Hollis's bedroom.

Sikya was lying on the bed. She burst into tears at the sight of her sister.

Shada rushed to her bedside. "Are you all right?" Shada asked.

"I'm fine," she said as she wiped tears from her eyes. "Just thankful to see you."

"They didn't hurt you, did they?"

"No, they've been taking care of me."

"Told you she was fine," Alfie said, inside Shada's head.

"They left you alone down here?"

"A nurse comes a few times a day to check on me. She makes sure everything's all right and brings more food. Sometimes there are other people in the main area, but I just stay in here."

Shada leaned over and gave her sister a hug.

"Can we go back to the city?" Sikya asked when they parted. "These people give me the creeps. They're so cold. I don't know how you spend so much time around them."

"You get used to it," Shada said. "And yes, we'll get you back to the city."

Shada heard the clunk of something heavy being placed on the table outside the bedroom. "There are just a few things I need to take care of," she said. She walked out of the room and told the men to move the prototype into the upload room. She took a deep breath before walking into the room herself.

The glare on Gustavo's face told Shada the edited mind was still in charge of her friend's body. Not a word was spoken while the storage device was set up.

"The electrodes need to be attached to your head," Shada said. "Are you going to make me order them to hold you down?"

Gustavo looked at the others in the room and the few peeking in from outside. He shook his head no.

At a nod from Shada, one of the men stuck an electrode to each of Gustavo's temples. Shada selected S for storage, then R. Gustavo had the look of a man who would commit murder if given the chance.

The countdown began. Shada hoped with everything she had that the edited mind inside her friend didn't know to allow the real Gustavo to regain control of his own body, which would make the unedited mind the one that got uploaded. When the countdown ended, Gustavo's body went limp.

CHAPTER TWENTY-NINE

SECONDS TICKED BY, then a full minute. Shada ordered everybody out of the room. When Gustavo opened his eyes, he looked at Shada and began uttering apologies with tears in his eyes.

"I couldn't take back control," he said.

Shada knew her friend was back. She walked to his side and laid a hand on his shoulder. "It's all right. You never have to go through that again."

Gustavo nodded, his breath catching in his chest. When he collected himself, he asked about the others. "Where are they? Are they all right?"

Shada told him she'd left them behind before she went to the lab. "I'll send some of the WestCorp employees outside to bring them here," she said, gesturing with her head to the door.

Gustavo's eyes searched Shada's face for an explanation as to why anyone from WestCorp would listen to her.

Shada walked to the door and stuck her head outside the room. She told the men to go to the dream stations, that her friends would be waking up soon. "There are three of them, two women and a man. Bring them here when they get out of the pods."

The men nodded.

"They won't want to come. Tell them Shada wants them to come to the bunker."

The men told Shada they'd be back soon and left.

"They think I'm Ruby," Shada turned and said to a stunned Gustavo. She then gave him a rough version of the events in Alfie's lab, finishing with the fact that she now had Alfie inside her and that Ruby, Marnie, Hollis, and the edited mind inside Gustavo were now trapped in the storage device.

Sikya, Shada, and Gustavo all sat down together to wait for the other three members of the resistance to turn up. Half of the WestCorp forces were there with them, and half were gone collecting the others. The elevator doors opened, and heavy footsteps could be heard walking down the corridor. All three of the unedited turned, hoping to see their comrades. Two oversized humans, the island's guards, emerged into the large space at the end of the corridor. Shada sent them away, saying their services were no longer required. They shrugged, turned around, and left.

Tony, Sophie, and Ophelia showed up an hour later. They seemed skeptical of their situation until they saw Shada, Sikya, and Gustavo sitting at the long table. Within moments they had crossed the space and embraced their friends. The looks of suspicion on the faces of the WestCorp employees disappeared with a stern look from Shada.

"What happened?" Tony said. "I could've killed you when I got out of that machine," he added, laughing.

Shada told them she would fill them in soon. "There's something we have to do first." She took each of them into the upload room one at a time and, after instructing them to give up control of their bodies during the countdown, put all the edited minds from their bodies into the device.

Once everyone but Shada was back to being the sole consciousness inside their bodies, she took them into Hollis's bedroom and shut the door. Inside, she told them about the events that had transpired in Alfie's lab.

"This is the second time I've heard this, and I still can't believe it," Gustavo said.

Tony was seated next to Sikya with his arm around her. "So now you're in charge of WestCorp," he said. "What's the first thing you're going to do?"

Shada thought for a moment. Then, frantic, she said she'd meant to stop the edits. "I can't believe I didn't remember!" she said. She rushed out of the bedroom and told the WestCorp employees to send the unedited back to the city. Inside her head, she asked Alfie how she would get a message out to those who had already been edited.

"There's a communications office," Alfie responded through thought.

Shada issued more instructions to the WestCorp employees. "Send someone to the communications office. Tell them I want everyone who was edited to come back to have the process reversed."

She hoped nobody had been edited in the short time she had been in charge. In her attempts to get to her sister and save her friends, she had forgotten one of the reasons she came to the island in the first place.

Alfie offered comfort. "Without me or Ruby telling them to start the edits back up after the lab was evacuated, nobody would take the initiative," he said.

Shada said she hoped that was the case.

Later that night, she found out Alfie was right. Everyone who had been in the lab when it was evacuated had stayed outside or gone back to the atrium. Since no edits were being completed, no one was sent back to the city, and no new unedited people had arrived.

Shada, Sikya, Gustavo, Tony, Sophie, and Ophelia ate dinner together then spent the night in the bunker. Tony and Sikya stayed in Hollis's bedroom, and Shada made space for herself in Hollis's study. Gustavo tried to sleep next to Shada, but she told him to stay on the other side of the room. She had no idea where Sophie and Ophelia slept.

Everyone left the bunker together the next morning. The morning sunlight reflected off the water surrounding the island. The air was crisp compared to the recycled air in the bunker. Jax the dog ran up to Shada's side and nudged Shada's hand with his gray beard.

"Get these fences taken down," Shada said to the guards posted outside.

They nodded. When they didn't move, she added, "Now," and they scrambled to disassemble the enclosure.

Jax joined the group, delighted to be outside the enclosure. They walked to the atrium, enjoying the sunshine, instead of taking a transport vehicle. The dog stopped at the entrance of the building when the humans walked inside. When Shada snapped her fingers, he hesitated before running to her side.

The space was full of unedited waiting to get back to the city. Undercurrents of anger swept through the crowd because they were going back without being edited. Everyone stared at the dog at Shada's side.

Shada and her group paused at the top of the stairs that led down to the tram.

"I'll come visit when I can," Shada said to the group.

Sikya stared at her sister in disbelief. "You're not coming back to the city with us?" she said.

"I've got to figure out what to do with this island and everyone on it. I'll be back soon."

Gustavo looked more pained than the others but nodded his agreement with the rest.

Sikya gave Shada a hug. "You'd better be there when the baby comes," she said.

"I wouldn't miss it," replied Shada.

The group split, leaving Shada at the top of the stairs. Jax, thinking everyone was going down, ran to the bottom and stood with his tail wagging while watching the group of humans descend. His tail stopped when he realized Shada was still at the top of the stairs. He paused for a moment before racing back up.

Together, Shada and Jax watched her sister and friends disappear into the crowd on the platform.

CHAPTER THIRTY

Shada looked at the city from her office. Fog covered the bases of the buildings, making the spires atop the skyscrapers seem like they were floating among the clouds. She had been in charge of the company for weeks.

At first, she'd wanted to dissolve the company once the edits of those terrorizing the city had been reversed. But collecting the edited had proved difficult. None of them trusted the company to reverse the procedure, and pockets of resistance dedicated to fighting WestCorp had sprung up all over.

When she had first heard about these groups, she'd laughed, thinking about how history had repeated itself. Now she was sad knowing her company was the object of their scorn when she was trying to help them. She wondered if Ruby had ever felt the same way.

The computer engineer who'd solved the storage problem walked into the office to tell her he had figured out a way to store the minds outside the one prototype. He told her he could store thousands on a server located on the island, and that they could be accessed anywhere connected to the island's network.

Shada asked if there was any way the stored minds could affect the island's other systems.

The engineer assured her they were useless outside of a body. "I made an alternate reality for them; they don't even know they're on a machine."

"Like a permanent dream station," Shada said.

"All I did was scale those up," the engineer replied.

Shada thought for a moment. "Do you think there's a way to get one of them a new body?" she asked the engineer. The thought of leaving Marnie in a reality with Michael and Ruby Hollis was repulsive.

"You want to upload them? Into who, other people from the city?"

"Not who. What. Androids."

The engineer thought for a moment. "You'd have to get other scientists involved. I don't know the first thing about robotics."

"But is it even possible?"

"I can't say for sure. What I can say is that it would take a long time, even with all the company's resources."

Inside Shada's head, Alfie said they should go for it. "Shada, this is the next step. Think about all the unedited people you could save. Their minds could live on the server after they die, and they could get into an android once we've perfected the technology."

Shada knew the first person she'd upload into an android would be Marnie. She told the engineer to take the steps necessary to begin the project.

"Will do . . . Mrs, Wes—er, Hollis."

Shada didn't miss the slip. Everyone on the island had gone from reporting to an aging Caucasian woman to taking orders from a young woman of color. She had heard the rumors, that her employees were calling her "Mrs. West" among themselves, but this was the first time anyone had used the name in person with her.

"I'm going to have everyone call me Ms. West," Shada said aloud, more to herself and Alfie than to the engineer.

The engineer looked embarrassed. "I'm sorry, I didn't mean anything by it."

"I'm serious, you can call me Ms. West."

"OK, Ms. West." The words seemed strange on his tongue. "Do you need anything else?"

Alfie laughed. Shada was the one person who could hear him. "You really want to be called Ms. West all the time? Like some teacher?"

"I don't want them to call me Shada, I know that much," Shada thought.

"So come up with a new name," Alfie said.

Shada, having just thought about Marnie, weighed the name on her tongue to see if it would work for herself. It didn't fit. "Barbie?" she thought. "Barnie?"

The computer engineer stared at her while her eyes searched the room, looking for her new first name.

"Marnie," she thought again. "Mable. Marble." Something clicked, and Shada focused on the engineer. "Amanda. Call me Amanda. First name basis from now on."

"Amanda West," Alfie said. "Has a nice ring to it."

Later that night, Shada wondered if it would ever be possible to duplicate consciousness. She was in the bunker, lying in what used to be Hollis's bed, and she wished she could have an android get her a glass of water. But if someone else's mind was inside the android, she would never be able to trust the machine. It would have to be her own consciousness, an exact copy, or as close as she could produce.

But if she did create the duplicate, what would happen when she died and her consciousness was uploaded onto the server? Would the duplicate be deleted? Absorbed? She felt a pang of jealousy for the duplicate that didn't even exist yet. It could rest and she couldn't.

This thought stuck in Shada's head as she drifted off to sleep.

Unedited minds would exist for eternity after they were uploaded. The edited, who had no problem with death and would therefore be uninterested in uploading their consciousnesses, would expire, never to exist again.

Were the edited the lucky ones?

Letting someone live and giving someone life are not the same.

INTERESTED IN READING MORE?

Find out more about the world Amanda West creates in *The Hysteria of Bodalís*! It's set in the distant future and based on the same mind-uploading technology Shada Gray/Amanda West experienced.

Get a copy FOR FREE by heading over to my website and subscribing to my email list.

authormarcoshernandez.com

Also, please help other readers learn more about this book by leaving a rating and review!

ABOUT THE AUTHOR

Marcos Antonio Hernandez writes from the suburbs of Washington, D.C. An avid reader of both fiction and non-fiction, his favorite authors are Haruki Murakami and Philip K. Dick — in that order.

Marcos graduated from the University of Maryland, College Park with a degree in chemical engineering and a minor in physics. Since graduating, he has worked as a barista, a food scientist, and a CrossFit coach.

Absolution is Marcos's sixth novel.

authormarcoshernandez.com